"I know it must have looked as if I was throwing myself at you, but it was quite accidental. I just lost my balance." Nicola felt her face flame.

"Really?" Dominic drawled. His cynical expression told her clearly that he didn't believe a word of it. "So you're saying it wasn't a come-on?"

"That's exactly what I'm saying."

He smiled grimly. "I suppose next you'll be swearing you didn't want to go to bed with me, and trying to blame me for seducing you?"

"I've no intention of trying to blame you for seducing me. I did want to go to bed with you."

Dominic raised a dark, mocking eyebrow. "Tell me, Nicola, do you feel the urge to sleep with every new man you meet?"

LEE WILKINSON lives with her husband in a three-hundred-year-old stone cottage in an English village, which most winters gets cut off by snow. They both enjoy traveling and recently, joining forces with their daughter and son-in-law, spend a year going around the world "on a shoestring" while their son looked after Kelly, their much-loved German shepherd dog. Lee's hobbies are reading and gardening and holding impromptu barbeques for her long-suffering family and friends.

Books by Lee Wilkinson

HARLEQUIN PRESENTS®
2228—MARRIAGE ON THE AGENDA
2264—A VENGEFUL DECEPTION

Don't miss any of our special offers. Write to us at the following address for information on our newest releases.

Harlequin Reader Service
U.S.: 3010 Walden Ave., P.O. Box 1325, Buffalo, NY 14269
Canadian: P.O. Box 609, Fort Erie, Ont. L2A 5X3

Lee Wilkinson

THE VENETIAN'S PROPOSAL

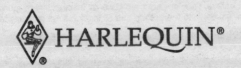

HARLEQUIN®

TORONTO • NEW YORK • LONDON
AMSTERDAM • PARIS • SYDNEY • HAMBURG
STOCKHOLM • ATHENS • TOKYO • MILAN • MADRID
PRAGUE • WARSAW • BUDAPEST • AUCKLAND

ISBN 0-373-18808-0

THE VENETIAN'S PROPOSAL

First North American Publication 2003.

Copyright © 2002 by Lee Wilkinson.

This edition published by arrangement with Harlequin Books S.A.

® and TM are trademarks of the publisher. Trademarks indicated with
® are registered in the United States Patent and Trademark Office, the
Canadian Trade Marks Office and in other countries.

Visit us at www.eHarlequin.com

Printed in U.S.A.

CHAPTER ONE

'PLEASE come in and take a seat, Mrs Whitney.'

Tall and slender in a navy suit, her corn-coloured hair taken up in a smooth knot, Nicola found herself ushered into a room that was solidly old-fashioned. Plum-coloured carpets, heavy velvet curtains, and above an empty fireplace a wooden mantel that held a ticking clock.

After coffee and condolences, Mr Harthill got down to business. 'The last time my client was in London he asked me to draw up a new will. In my capacity as executor, I can now tell you that you are the sole beneficiary of that will.'

Staring across a polished mahogany desk at the saggy-jowled solicitor sitting impassively in his brown leather chair, Nicola could only manage to stutter, 'I—I beg your pardon?'

'You are the sole beneficiary,' Mr Harthill Senior repeated patiently. 'When all the formalities have been observed, you will be a wealthy woman.'

A polite letter summoning Nicola to the West End offices of Harthill, Harthill and Berry had merely stated that Mr John Turner had passed away some three weeks earlier, and that if she would call she would learn 'something to her advantage'.

Shocked and saddened by the death of a man she had known for such a short time but liked immensely, she had kept the appointment.

The news that John Turner had made her the sole beneficiary to a fortune she hadn't been aware existed had come as a bombshell.

'But why me?' She spoke the thought aloud.

'I gather that Mr Turner didn't have any children of his own…'

No, John had never mentioned having a family.

'As well as his business interests,' Mr Harthill continued staidly, 'my client's estate includes the proceeds from the sale of his London home, and a small *palazzo* in Venice, known as Ca' Malvasia. He and his wife were very happy there, I understand.'

The London house Nicola had known about. John had mentioned his intention of putting it on the market, saying it was too big and too empty and he was hardly ever there. But his 'small *palazzo*' in Venice she hadn't. Though she was aware that John's deceased wife, Sophia, had been Italian.

'Is that where he died?' was all she could think of to ask.

Mr Harthill, used to euphemisms and looking a little distressed by her plain speaking, answered, 'No. Ca' Malvasia has been shut up since his wife passed away some four years ago. My client was in Rome on business when he suffered a fatal heart attack…'

She hoped someone had been with him. That he hadn't died alone.

'It wasn't totally unexpected,' the solicitor went on, 'and he had made provision. In the event of his death I was to give you this package, which I believe holds a set of keys to the *palazzo*.'

He handed her a small, thick envelope sealed with tape which bore her name and the address of the Bayswater flat she shared with her friend Sandy.

'If you wish to view the property I can put you in touch with my Venetian counterpart, Signor Mancini, who has been the family's solicitor for a number of years. He will be only too happy to help with your travel arrangements and show you the *palazzo*. Should you decide to sell, he can take the appropriate measures to have it put on the market.'

Sounding as dazed as she felt, Nicola said, 'I'll need to make some plans...take time off work.'

'Of course.' Mr Harthill rose to his feet to show her out. 'If I can be of any further service in the meantime, please let me know.'

'Thank you. You've been very kind.' She smiled at him. A smile that brought warmth to her heart-shaped face and lit up her green eyes.

A beautiful woman, he thought as they shook hands, and tragically young to be a widow. Even a rich one.

When Nicola let herself into the flat Sandy, a small vivacious redhead, was waiting, agog with excitement.

'I've made some tea. Come and tell all.'

Friends since their days at business college, and flatmates for the past three years, the pair were complete opposites. One an introvert. The other an extrovert.

Even before her young husband's fatal car crash Nicola had been quiet and self-contained, a woman who tended to stand alone in the wings and watch.

Whereas Sandy, outgoing and outspoken, was at her best bouncing off people.

In what seemed to be a case of role-reversal Sandy worked from home, as an information consultant, sitting in front of a computer screen in what she described as solitary confinement, while Nicola liaised with people, travelling almost non-stop as a conference organizer for Westlake Business Solutions.

Together they went through to the bright little kitchen and sat down at the pine table, where Sandy poured tea for them both.

Nicola accepted a mug and said simply, 'John made me his sole beneficiary. It seems I'm going to be a wealthy woman.'

Sandy gave a silent whistle.

'Apart from his business interests and the money from the sale of his London house, there's also a small *palazzo* in Venice.'

'You're joking!'

'No, I'm not.'

'Did you know he had a place in Venice?'

'No, he never mentioned it.'

'Sure you haven't got it wrong?'

'Certain. It's called Ca' Malvasia. I've even been given a set of keys to it.'

Taking the padded envelope from her bag, Nicola tore off the tape and tipped the contents on to the table.

As well as a bunch of ornate keys on an iron ring there was a small chamois pouch with a drawstring neck and a letter.

While Sandy examined the keys, Nicola unfolded the letter and read in John's small, neat writing:

Nicola, my dear, though we've known each other just a short time, you've been like the daughter I always wanted, and your warmth and kindness have meant a lot to me.

In the pouch you'll find Sophia's ring. Since she died I've been wearing it on a chain around my neck, but now I sense that I haven't got much longer I'm lodging it with Mr Harthill.

It's a singular ring. My darling always wore it. She was wearing it the day I met her. She once remarked that if any ring possessed the power to bring its wearer happiness, this one did. For that reason I would like you to have it, and I truly believe Sophia would approve.

Though we had both been married before, she was the love of my life as, I hope and believe, I was hers. We were very happy together for five wonderful years. Not long enough. But perhaps it never is.

In your case, I know your time with your husband was very brief. You're desperately young to have known so much grief and pain, and I'm only too aware that anyone who loses a loved one needs time to mourn. But remember, my dear, no one should mourn for ever. It's time you moved on. Be happy.

John

Blinking away her tears, Nicola passed the letter to Sandy, and, while the other girl read it quickly, picked up the chamois pouch and unfastened the drawstring. Tilting the pouch, she gave it a slight shake, and a ring slid into her palm.

Both women caught their breath.

It was exquisitely wrought, with twin ovals of glittering green stone sunk at an angle in the softly glowing gold setting.

'I've never seen anything like it.' Sandy's face held awe. 'What's it meant to be?'

Her voice unsteady, Nicola said, 'It looks like a gold mask, with emeralds for eyes.'

'Try it on,' Sandy urged.

With a strange feeling of doing something portentous, Nicola slid it on to her finger.

After Jeff's death she had lost weight to the point of becoming gaunt, and it was just a fraction too large.

'Even if it's only costume jewellery it looks fantastic!' Sandy enthused. 'Though it may be a little too spectacular to wear to the local supermarket.'

'You're right,' Nicola agreed. 'It would look more at home in Piazza San Marco.'

'Are you going to wear it?'

'At the moment I'd be scared of losing it. But I'll certainly keep it with me.'

'You speak Italian, don't you? Have you ever been to Venice?'

'No.'

'Wouldn't you like to go?'

'Yes, I would,' Nicola said slowly. 'I was thinking about it on the way home. I've time owing to me, so I might take a holiday. Stay there for a while.'

'Glory be!' Sandy exclaimed. 'A sign of life at last. I'd about given up hope. You haven't had a holiday since Jeff was killed.'

'There didn't seem much point. It's no fun staying in a hotel full of strangers. In any case, it's too much like work.'

'But you won't need to stay in a hotel when you have your very own *palazzo*.'

Nicola half shook her head. 'I can still hardly believe it.'

Her smooth forehead wrinkling into a frown, Sandy remarked curiously, 'I wonder why John Turner never mentioned having a house in Venice?'

'Talking about it might have conjured up too many ghosts. He absolutely adored his wife, and couldn't get over her death. It's one of the reasons he worked so hard and travelled so much...'

Nicola had done the same, only to find that pain and grief couldn't be left behind. They had travelled with her, constant companions she had been unable to outstrip.

Though she'd never found it particularly easy to make friends, she and John Turner had met and, drawn together by circumstances and their mutual loss, become firm friends—overnight, almost. The immediacy of their friendship had never been discussed or questioned, just accepted.

'Though there was an age difference of over thirty years, John and I had a lot in common. I was very fond of him.

I'll miss him.' With a lump in her throat, she added, 'I'd like to see the house where he and his wife were so happy.'

'Well, now's your chance.' Sandy's tone was practical. 'Why don't you come with me?'

'I can't say I'm not tempted, but I've too much work on. Besides, Brent would hate me to go to Venice without him. Apart from believing that English women find all Italian men fascinating, he thinks Italian men tend to stare at English women... And while he might not mind them *looking*, if it came to bottom-pinching...'

'I rather hope it won't.'

'You should be so lucky!' Sandy said with a grin. 'So how will you travel? Fly, as usual?'

'I'm tired of flying, seeing nothing but airports...' With a sudden determination to lay her own ghosts, Nicola decided, 'I think I'll drive down...'

Jeff, who had been the elder by six months or so, had passed his own driving test and taught her to drive in a small family saloon when she was just seventeen. But since his death she hadn't driven.

'In early June the weather should be good, so I think I'll plan a scenic route and take a leisurely trip, stopping three or four nights on the way. I'd love to see Innsbruck.'

Hiding her surprise, Sandy observed, 'While not wishing to spoil your fun, I must point out that you don't have a car.'

'I can always hire one.'

'And I've heard the price of parking in Venice is astronomical. But I don't suppose you need to worry about it now. By the way, now you've money to burn I expect you'll want to live somewhere a bit more up-market?'

Before Nicola could answer, she added, 'Don't think I'm trying to push you off, but Brent is itching to move in. I've kept the poor lamb waiting because I wasn't sure how you'd feel about having an extra flatmate, and a man to boot.'

'So you've decided to live together?'

'For a trial period. If it works out we may get married. Brent would like to.'

'Well, let me know if you want to spend your honeymoon in a *palazzo*...'

Without envy, Sandy said cheerfully, 'I do like having rich friends.'

Signor Mancini, when notified of Nicola's intentions, had proved almost embarrassingly eager to be of assistance. Though she had assured him that it wasn't necessary, he had advised her where to stay, and gallantly insisted on making all the hotel bookings.

For some reason, and without ever hearing his voice, Sandy had taken a dislike to the man. She now called him 'the slimy git'. But, unwilling to hurt his feelings, Nicola had thanked him and, abandoning her busman's holiday, accepted his well-meant help.

The only thing she had vetoed was that he should meet her on her arrival in Venice and personally conduct her to the hotel.

There was really no need to take up his valuable time, she had insisted politely, and it would tie her to being there at a certain hour.

Her last planned stop before Venice was Innsbruck, and she arrived in the picturesque Austrian city in the early afternoon.

Signor Mancini had arranged for her to stay at the Bregenzerwald, a nice-looking modern hotel just off the impressive Maria-Theresien-Strasse.

Nicola parked her hired car in the underground car park and, leaving her main suitcase in the boot, collected her small overnight bag and took the lift up to the elegant foyer.

It was deserted at that time of the day, except for the

desk-clerk and a thick-necked, bullet-headed man sitting by the window, who glanced up at her approach.

Having studied her for a moment, he retired once more behind his newspaper while she completed the formalities and was handed her room key.

It was her first visit to the capital of the Tyrol and, liking Innsbruck on sight, she decided to see as much as she possibly could in the relatively short time at her disposal.

As soon as she had showered and changed into a cream linen dress and jacket she made her way down to the foyer again, to find the same man was still sitting there, intent on his newspaper.

Having collected a street map from the desk, she turned to go.

The bullet-headed man had abandoned his paper and, his gaze fixed on her, was talking into a mobile phone. Their eyes met briefly, and perhaps embarrassed to be caught staring—even absently—he instantly looked away.

Map in hand, Nicola made her way into the sunny street, and after getting her bearings set off to explore.

There were plenty of horse-drawn carriages offering sightseeing tours, but, needing to stretch her legs following the day's drive, she decided to walk.

The sky was cloudless, the sun warm enough to make her push up the sleeves of her jacket, but traces of snow were still visible on the surrounding Alps.

After a look at the milky-green, fast-flowing Inn river, she made her way to the old part of town. The Altstadt, with its famous golden-roofed balcony and bulbous-domed Stadtturm tower, was colourful and bustling with tourists.

Strolling through the narrow, cobbled lanes, she was stepping back to admire one of the painted buildings when the thin heel of her court shoe slipped into a crack between the smooth stones and wedged tightly.

As she struggled to free it she heard the clatter of approaching hooves bearing down on her.

A second later she was swept up by a pair of strong arms and whisked to safety, while the horse-drawn carriage rattled harmlessly past.

For a moment or two, shaken, she lay with her head supported by a muscular shoulder, vaguely aware of the feel of silk beneath her cheek and the fresh masculine scent of cologne.

Then, pulling herself together, she raised her head and said a trifle unsteadily, 'Thank you. Believe me, I'm very grateful.'

'It was, perhaps, unnecessarily dramatic…' His voice was attractive, well-educated, his English perfect with only the faintest trace of an accent. 'But I'm glad I was on hand.'

Her rescuer was darkly handsome, without being swarthy, and just looking into his face took what was left of her breath away.

Apart from the colour of his eyes, he was a lot like her husband. Jeff's eyes had been a warm, cloudy blue, whereas this man's were a cool, clear grey. His hair was thick and raven-black—cut just short enough to restrain its desire to curl—his face lean and hard-boned, with a straight nose and a firm, chiselled mouth.

As she stared at him as though mesmerised, he said, 'Now I'd better retrieve your footwear.'

Setting her down carefully, so she could lean against the plastered wall of a building, he stepped out into the roadway.

He was tall and broad-shouldered and moved with an easy, masculine grace. Well, but casually dressed, in stone-coloured trousers and an open-necked shirt, he could have been simply a holidaymaker.

But there was something indefinable about him—a kind

of sureness? An air of authority?—that convinced her he wasn't.

Having eased the shoe free, he carried it back. 'The heel's a little scuffed, but apart from that it's undamaged.'

Settling on his haunches, he slipped the court shoe on to her slender foot, before straightening to his full height—some six feet plus.

Looking down at her heart-shaped face, with its pure bone structure and flawless skin, he commented, 'You still look shaken...'

She was. But not for the reason he imagined.

'What you need is that panacea for all ills, a nice cup of tea.'

His hand beneath her elbow, he led her round a corner to the Stadsbiesl, a tiny restaurant with overhanging eaves and white stucco walls. Its tiled roof sloping every which way, the old building leaned, supported like an amiable drunk between its neighbours.

A tunnelled archway gave access to a small sunny court-yard with three or four unoccupied tables covered with red-checked tablecloths.

'But perhaps, as you're fair-skinned, you'd prefer to be indoors?' he asked.

She shook her head. 'I love the sun and, so long as I don't do anything foolish, I tan quite easily.'

'Then al fresco it is.'

He helped her off with her linen jacket and hung it over the back of her chair.

The moment they were seated a white-coated waiter appeared with a pitcher of iced water and two glasses.

'Just tea?' Nicola's companion enquired. 'Or would you like to try a plate of the delectable cakes they serve here?'

'I had a late lunch, so just hot tea with lemon, thank you.'

He gave the order in fluent German, though she felt sure it wasn't his native tongue.

As the waiter moved away she remarked, 'You seem to know the Stadsbiesl well?'

'Yes. I eat here from time to time.' Studying her, he added, 'Your colour's coming back. Feeling better?'

'Much better.'

'On holiday?'

'Yes.'

'Is this your first time in Innsbruck?'

'Yes.' Reluctantly, she added, 'Though I'm only staying for one night. I'm on my way to Venice.'

'From England?'

'Yes. I'm driving down. Taking the scenic route.'

'It's a magnificent run over the Brenner Pass.'

'I'm sure it must be. I'm looking forward to it.'

But not so much as she had been.

Their pot of tea arrived, strings and tags dangling from beneath the lid. It was accompanied by a silver bowl of sugar cubes and another of thinly sliced lemon. On each bowl there was a pair of silver tongs shaped like twin dragons joined at the tail.

Indicating the pot, he suggested, 'Perhaps you'll pour?'

'Of course. Lemon and sugar?'

'Just lemon, please.'

She filled both cups, and passed him one. Then, made unusually clumsy by the knowledge that he was studying her, she dropped a piece of lemon into her own, so that it splashed tea down the bodice of her dress.

Getting to his feet, he felt in his pocket and produced an immaculate handkerchief. He dipped the corner into the pitcher of water and leaned over her to rub gently at the orange-brown stains.

Though his touch was light and impersonal, every nerve-ending in her body responded, and she felt her cheeks grow hot.

He moved back and, his head tipped a little to one side,

studied the results of his ministrations. 'There are still one or two faint marks but nothing too obvious.'

'Thank you,' she said in a strangled voice.

'It was my pleasure entirely,' he responded, straight-faced.

Uncertain whether or not he was laughing at her, she gathered herself, and, needing a topic of conversation, asked a shade breathlessly, 'Do you live in Innsbruck?'

'No, I'm here on business.' His eyes on her face, he went on, 'I live in Venice.'

'Oh…' For no reason at all, her heart lifted.

Still watching her, as though he was half expecting some reaction, he added deliberately, 'My name's Loredan… Dominic Irving Loredan.'

'Are you Italian?' was all she could think of to say.

'Half. My father was from the States, but my mother was Italian.'

So that accounted for the faint and fascinating accent she had noticed, and also for the eloquent way he used his long well-shaped hands when he was speaking.

'You're English, I take it?'

'Yes. I'm Nicola Whitney.'

He glanced at her wedding ring. '*Mrs* Whitney, I see.'

'Yes… No… Well, yes…'

Raising a dark winged brow, he commented, 'You seem a little uncertain.'

'I—I'm a widow,' she stammered.

Perhaps afraid of pitying exclamations, or maybe because to say it aloud made it all too real, this was only the second time she had voluntarily admitted her widowhood.

'You're very young to be a widow,' he remarked evenly.

'I'm twenty-five.'

'When did your husband die?'

'Three years ago.'

'And you're still wearing your ring?'

She still felt married.

When she said nothing, he pursued, 'Was his death some kind of accident?'

Because his question was matter-of-fact, unemotional, she was able to answer steadily, 'Yes. He was killed in a car crash.'

'So you're on your own?'

'I share a flat with a friend, Sandy.'

'He's not holidaying with you?'

'No, I'm alone… And Sandy's a *she*.'

Now why had she found it necessary to tell a complete stranger that? she wondered. Other people had made the same mistake and she hadn't bothered to correct them.

More than a little flustered, she hurried on, 'We met at college, and after Jeff, my husband, died she invited me to share her flat. I would have liked her to come with me, but she's a self-employed information consultant and she had too much work on.'

His manner casual, he queried, 'Are you in the same line of business?'

'No. I work for Westlake Business Solutions as a conference organiser.'

'Sounds very impressive. Are you good at your job?'

'Yes.'

The gleam in his grey eyes showed his appreciation of her answer before he asked, 'What qualifications are necessary for a job like that? Apart from looks?'

As he added the rider there seemed to be a slight edge to his voice. Or was she just imagining it?

She answered briefly, 'No qualifications as such.'

'Then what *do* you need?'

'A knowledge of how business works, a flair for judging what different clients want, and a certain originality. The ability to speak at least one extra language fluently is useful.'

'And do you? Speak another language, I mean?'

'Yes.'

'Do go on,' he said smoothly.

She shrugged slender shoulders. 'On the whole it's just hard work. Organising accommodation, conference facilities, a supply of suitable food and drink etcetera, and making sure everyone's happy.'

'Which I'm sure you do wonderfully well.'

This time there was no doubt about the edge, and, biting her lip, she remained silent.

'So where do you organise these conferences?'

'Worldwide...Tokyo, Sydney, Atlanta, Quebec, Paris, London.'

'That must involve a great deal of travelling.'

'Yes, it does.'

'And a good chance to meet people? The business delegates, for example?'

Disconcerted by his manner, and feeling a growing tension, she answered awkwardly, 'I usually only get to meet the people actually attending the conference, if things aren't going smoothly.'

'And of course you make sure they are?'

'As far as possible.'

Apparently sensing her discomfort, he sighed, and, leaning back in his chair, shook his head ruefully. 'Forgive me. I hope you'll accept my apologies?'

'For what?'

He gave a charming grimace. 'I shouldn't be grilling you about your life and work. You're on holiday and the sun's shining.'

The feeling of tension disappeared as though it had never existed.

And perhaps it hadn't. Maybe it had been all in her mind? Something to do with his resemblance to Jeff? Or the fact that for the past three years she had avoided socialising in this way, and so had lost her ability to mix and relax on a personal level?

'What do you have planned for the rest of your day in Innsbruck?' His low, clear voice broke into her thoughts.

'As much sightseeing as possible.'

'Alone?'

'Well, yes.'

'As my business is now successfully underway, and I'm alone too, perhaps you'll allow me to show you around?'

Her heart picked up speed and began to beat a tattoo against her ribcage while she decided what her answer should be.

She found him a fascinating and disturbing man. Disturbing not only because he reminded her of Jeff, but in a way she was unable to put her finger on.

Yet though her time spent in his company hadn't been altogether comfortable—and perhaps it was her own reaction to his explosive sex appeal that had caused her discomfort—she knew she didn't want it to end.

To hide the excitement that had suddenly made her feel like a girl again, she answered carefully, 'Thank you, that would be very nice.'

Whether he was amused by her primness, or pleased by her acceptance, she wasn't sure, but his white, even teeth flashed in a smile.

It was the first time she had seen him smile, and it added a thousandfold to his already considerable charm.

Dropping some *schillings* onto the table, he said, 'Then let's go.'

She gathered up her bag and jacket and they left the sunny courtyard, his hand at her waist.

Just that casual touch made her heart beat in a way that it had never done before. She had loved Jeff deeply, but they had been brought up together, he had been part of her life, so it had been a gentle, familiar caring. A feeling of warmth and safety rather than a mad excitement.

'Innsbruck is a compact city as far as sightseeing goes,' Dominic Loredan remarked as they emerged into the street. 'Almost everything of interest is here in the Altstadt—unless you'd like to see the Olympic ski jump, or the Europabrucke, Europe's highest bridge? Though tomorrow, if you head south on the motorway, you'll cross it.'

'I think, as time's limited, I'll stick with the historical part.'

'Then I suggest we start with the Hofburg Palace and the Hofkirche Chapel... That is, if you haven't already seen them...?'

'No, I haven't,' she said, no longer caring overmuch what she saw. Just being with this charismatic man was enough.

'They're just across the way from each other...'

His mouth was fascinating, she thought. It was a mouth that was at once coolly austere and warmly sensual. A clear-cut mouth that sent little shivers down her spine...

'Then later I'll take you up to Schloss Lienz for dinner.'

She dragged her gaze away from his mouth and, feeling her colour rise, echoed, 'Schloss Lienz?'

'The *schloss* dates from the sixteenth-century and has quite a turbulent history. To begin with it was a fortress, then it was used as a royal hunting lodge, now it's a first-class restaurant. From the terrace, which seems to hang in space, there's a superb view over the city.'

'It sounds wonderful.' Glancing down at the faint marks still visible on her dress, she added, 'Though I'll need to get changed first.'

'So will I. Where are you staying?'

'At the Bregenzerwald.'

'What a coincidence!'

'You mean you are?'

'Room 54.'

Hardly able to believe it, she marvelled, 'I'm in room 56.'

'Well, well... It seems coincidences are like swallows; they come in pairs...'

The rest of the afternoon passed in a haze of excitement. Nicola hadn't known this kind of happiness for over three years.

She found that Dominic Loredan was an easy and interesting companion, who proved to have an extensive knowledge of the city, an appreciation of beauty, and a dry sense of humour when pointing out the more droll aspects of the scenery.

When the pair had finally finished traipsing around the cobbled lanes of the old town, and seen most of what was to be seen, warm and a little dusty, they took a horse-drawn carriage back to their hotel.

Leaving her at her door, Dominic asked, 'How long will you need? An hour? Half an hour?'

Not having expected to dress up for dinner, she would have to go down to the car for her main suitcase. Even so...

'Just long enough to have a shower and get changed,' she answered quickly, begrudging even this amount of time spent away from him.

'Good.' Grey eyes smiled into green. 'I'll give you a knock in about half an hour.'

As she looked up at him he brushed her cheek with a single finger, and while she stood mesmerised, he bent his dark head and touched his lips to hers, a thistledown kiss that turned her knees to water and melted every last bone in her body.

Totally bemused, a hand to her lips, she watched him disappear into his own room. Then, like someone under a spell, she went into hers and gently closed the door.

CHAPTER TWO

FOR a little while she stood quite still, feeling again that most fleeting of caresses. Pulling herself together, she went to pick up her car keys.

Frowning, she stared at the empty space where she remembered them being before glancing around. Instead of lying on the chest of drawers, the keys, with their rental tag, were on the dressing table.

Perhaps she was mistaken? Maybe that was where she had left them? Or possibly one of the chambermaids had come in and moved them?

Whichever, the important thing was they were still there. So long as the car hadn't been stolen it wasn't a problem.

Stolen...

The implications of that thought made Nicola check her overnight case. A quick glance through the contents showed her passport and spare money were untouched, and so was her grandmother's jewellery box, which held most of the things she treasured.

Holding her breath, she released the catch and opened it. Everything seemed to be there. A small string of pearls Jeff had bought her for a wedding present, her grandmother's locket, the keys to John's house in Venice...

With a sigh of relief, she closed the lid and replaced the box.

Then, picking up the car keys, she took the lift down to the car park and hurried over to the blue saloon. Releasing the central locking, she moved to lift the lid of the boot.

It refused to budge.

Another press of the key released it. Which undoubtedly meant that it hadn't been locked in the first place.

Oh, but surely she'd locked it?

Or had she?

She lifted the boot lid, half expecting to see her case gone, but it was still there, exactly as she'd left it.

No, not *exactly*.

As if someone had closed it in a hurry, caught between the two zips where they met in the centre, was a small piece of material.

Opening the case, she looked inside. Once again nothing was missing. Everything seemed to be as it should be, apart from that tell-tale scrap of ivory satin that had been caught in the zip.

Eager to be off that morning, she had wasted no time in packing, so perhaps she had left that bit of nightdress hanging out?

But wouldn't she have noticed it?

Apparently not.

The only rational explanation had to be her own carelessness.

Yet the three things—the keys being moved, the car being unlocked, and the material caught between the zips—made a logical sequence that was very hard to dismiss.

Except that in the long run it made no sense.

If someone had got into her room and, finding the distinctive rental-tagged keys, gone to the trouble of locating the car and searching her case, wouldn't they have taken everything worth stealing? Including the car?

Instead there was nothing missing and the keys were still there. Which seemed to prove the whole thing was just a strange coincidence.

And coincidences did happen. Dominic Loredan being in the same hotel and having the room next to hers was proof of that.

Her thoughts having flown back to Dominic and the evening ahead, she lifted out the case, locked the car and hurried over to the lift.

Once in her room, having showered in record time, she donned fresh undies and a smoke-grey silk chiffon dress that Sandy had nagged her into buying, saying, 'You never know…'

It was a romantic dress, with a cross-over bodice, a long, swirling skirt and a matching stole. Shaking out the stole, which was lined with scarlet, Nicola hesitated, still unsure.

But recalling how, when she had hesitated at the colour, Sandy had exclaimed crossly, 'Oh, for heaven's sake! You can't go on wearing widow's weeds for ever', she made up her mind to take it.

Placing it on a chair with her small evening bag, she stood in front of the mirror to take up her thick, naturally blonde hair.

As she held the smooth coil in place on top of her head and began to push in the pins her eyes were drawn to her wedding ring.

Her task finished, she studied the thin gold band. Married for barely a year when Jeff was killed, she had now been a widow for considerably longer than she had been a wife.

As John had said, anyone who had lost a loved one needed to mourn, but no one should mourn for ever.

Maybe the time had come to let go of the past.

Slipping off the ring, she put it carefully with her other treasures.

Anxious to look her best—for the first time in more than three years—she picked up her cosmetic case and turned back to the mirror.

With somewhat darker brows and lashes, and a clear skin, she needed very little in the way of make-up. A dab of powder to stop her small straight nose from shining, a touch of green eyeshadow and a light coating of pale lipgloss and she was ready.

A knock made her snatch up her evening bag and stole and hurry to open the door.

Looking devastatingly handsome in a black tie and evening jacket, Dominic Loredan was waiting.

His gaze travelled over her from head to toe and back again, making her feel oddly shivery, before he remarked evenly, 'You really are the most beautiful thing I've ever seen.'

Just for an instant she had the odd impression that his words hadn't been intended as a compliment.

Perhaps he read the uncertainty in her face, because he took her hand and raised it to his lips.

The romantic little gesture and its accompanying smile smoothed away the impression, as the sea smoothed away footprints in the sand.

Her heart lifting, she returned his smile. 'I'm afraid I forgot to thank you for a lovely afternoon.'

Taking the stole from her, he put it around her shoulders and offered her his arm. 'The evening should prove to be even better.'

His sleek white sports car was waiting in the car park, its hood back, and in a matter of minutes they were making their way out of the city. Though the sun had gone, the air was still comfortably warm, and in the low-slung seats they were shielded from too much wind.

Soon they began to climb steadily, the view changing with every horseshoe bend. Stands of trees set in sloping green meadows... The flash of water and a roadside shrine bright with flowers... Wooden chalets, with a steepled church perched high on a bluff above them... Then, set against the magnificent backdrop of mountains, a turreted castle.

'The Schloss Lienz,' Dominic said.

'It's a real picture-book place,' she remarked delightedly.

'I'm pleased you like it,' he said gravely, as he took the winding road up to the *schloss*. When they reached it they drove through an archway into a vast cobbled courtyard. Set around it were metal sconces holding long torches that looked like enormous bulrushes.

Having helped Nicola out, he handed the car keys to a hovering attendant, and it was whisked through another archway, out of sight.

At this height the alpine air was appreciably cooler and fresher as she stood staring up at the grey stone walls towering above them. Seeing her slight shiver, Dominic thoughtfully adjusted her stole higher on her shoulders.

'Thank you.' She smiled at him, suddenly feeling cosseted and cared for, a feeling she hadn't experienced for a very long time.

At the entrance to the *schloss* they were greeted by a thick-set man with blond hair, who was, Nicola discovered later, the Baron Von Salzach.

In heavily accented English, he said, 'Good evening, Dominic. It is nice to see you again. Mrs Whitney, welcome to Schloss Lienz. If you will follow me, you have a table on the terrace, as requested.'

'Thank you, Franz.'

Their host led the way to the end of a large flagged hall and through a carpeted, chandelier-hung dining-room, where a quartet of musicians played Mozart and most of the well-dressed clientele seemed to be in decorous groups.

As they followed him Nicola noticed that several of the women with middle-aged escorts gave Dominic a second surreptitious glance, and her an envious one. As they reached a long, curving flight of stone stairs, Franz said, 'Please be careful. The steps are old and worn in places.'

The stairway led up to a flagged open-air terrace, which

held only a handful of widely spaced tables, four of which were already occupied.

'Out here it's somewhat less stuffy,' Dominic remarked *sotto voce*.

His sidelong smile convinced her he wasn't referring to the temperature.

When they were seated at a table set with gleaming crystal and a centrepiece of fresh flowers, the Baron said, 'I hope you will enjoy your meal,' clicked his heels, and departed.

Intrigued by the glowing charcoal braziers standing at intervals along the waist-high outer wall, Nicola remarked, 'They look so wonderfully appropriate.'

'As soon as the sun goes down they're necessary to keep the air comfortably warm,' Dominic explained. 'Though before they were installed, a couple of years ago, the hardy diner would risk pneumonia for the sake of the view.'

Gazing at the wonderful panorama of Innsbruck spread below them in the wide, flat valley of the Inn, she said, 'If you want my opinion, it was well worth the risk.'

'When all the city lights start to come on, you'll find it's even better.'

As they ordered and ate a superb dinner she found he was right. In the blue velvet dusk the glittering lights turned the twenty-first century into a fairy tale. While at the castle itself the lanterns on the terrace and the flaring torches in the courtyard below gave the scene a medieval feel.

Though he drank little himself, Dominic kept Nicola's glass topped up with an excellent Riesling that was light and subtle and easy to keep sipping.

Caught up in the magic of the moment, a magic that had a lot to do with the *schloss* but even more to do with her companion, she failed to notice just how much she was drinking.

During the meal he had steered clear of anything remotely personal, so it came as a complete surprise when, reaching across the table, he lifted her bare left hand and remarked, 'You've taken off your ring.'

'Yes.'

'Why?'

'I—I'm not sure,' she stammered, shaken both by his touch and his question. 'The time just seemed to be right.'

Something in his look made her go on to explain, 'I suddenly realised I'd been a widow for longer than I'd been a wife.'

Releasing her hand, he queried, 'How long were you married?'

'Not quite a year…'

Perhaps it was too much wine that loosened her tongue, or maybe, at long last, the time had come when she felt it a relief to be able to talk about the past.

Whichever, she found herself opening up to a perfect stranger in a way she hadn't been able to open up to anyone, except John.

'Jeff and I had a traditional white wedding on my twenty-first birthday.'

'But you'd lived together before that?'

'Virtually all our lives… Oh, I see what you mean. No, we hadn't lived together in that sense.'

Seeing his slight frown, she explained, 'Jeff's parents were my parents too. My *foster* parents. They had been my grandmother's friends for a number of years, and they took care of me while she was in hospital and after she died.'

'How old were you then?'

'Just turned five.'

'And your husband?'

'He was a few months older, and their only child.'

'They never tried to officially adopt you?'

'I think they would have liked to. They had hoped for more children, but they were well past middle-age when Jeff was born, so they would have been considered too old.'

'You had no grandfather?'

'He'd died the previous year.'

'What about your natural parents?'

'I'd never known them, and one day, having realised that most of my peers had a mummy and daddy, I asked my grandmother why *I* didn't. She sat me on her knee and gave me a cuddle while she explained that mine had gone away. Because of something one of my little friends had said, I translated ''gone away'' as ''gone to heaven'', and over the years my foster parents, no doubt thinking it was for the best, allowed me to go on believing they were dead.

'Then when I reached sixteen, perhaps as an awful warning, they decided I was old enough to know the truth. My natural mother, whose name was Helen, was my grandmother's only child. From the age of thirteen she'd been a bit wild, and she was barely sixteen when she discovered she was pregnant.

'It seems she wanted to have an abortion, but my grandmother was horrified and insisted on her going through with the pregnancy.

'She hated the whole idea of motherhood, and even before I was born blamed me for spoiling her life. When I was only a few weeks old she disappeared, leaving my grandmother to take care of me.'

'Your grandmother must have been quite young when she died?'

'She was in her middle fifties. She had some kind of minor operation that went tragically wrong.'

Running lean fingers over his smooth chin, Dominic remarked thoughtfully, 'So, with having the same parents, you and your husband must have been brought up like sister and brother?'

Made a little uncomfortable by the bluntness of the question, she answered, 'We were always very close. Though we spent most of our time together—we even went to the same school—we never argued or fell out… I can't ever remember not loving Jeff, and it was the same for him.' Smiling fondly, she added, 'He once told me he'd loved me since I was a scrawny five-year-old with big solemn eyes and a pigtail.'

'Didn't close friends think it strange that you never quarrelled like other siblings?'

She answered truthfully, 'I don't recall having a really close friend, apart from Jeff, until I got to college. As children, our parents didn't encourage us to mix much, and really we never seemed to need anyone else.'

'What about when you grew into adults?'

'You mean did we stay friends?'

'I mean when did you become lovers?'

'Jeff wanted us to sleep together as soon as I'd turned eighteen.'

'But you didn't?'

She shook her head. 'No… Though after he'd died I almost wished we had. It seemed such a waste of three years… But although our parents were kind, they were quite strict and God-fearing, and they seriously disapproved of anyone having sex outside marriage.'

'So what happened?'

'Jeff suggested we should get married, but we were due to start college and neither of us had any money. Eventually he decided to approach our parents and tell them we loved each other and wanted to be together.

'When he did, they said if we waited until we'd finished college—to be sure we weren't making a mistake—they would give us their blessing and pay for a white wedding and all the trimmings. That way they could be proud of us.'

Seeing Dominic's expression, she admitted, 'It must seem terribly old-fashioned, but we'd been brought up to respect their wishes, and living under their roof meant accepting their standards. Apart from anything else they'd been very good to me, and I didn't want to let them down, so finally we promised to wait.'

His grey eyes intent, Dominic asked, 'Surely a promise like that went by the board once you got into student accommodation?'

'The college was only just down the road, and in the circumstances it seemed sensible to keep on living at home.'

Dominic's flicker of a smile said it all.

Disturbed by that smile, she found herself defending the decision. 'It was what our parents wanted us to do. They said some of the students were a wild bunch and we'd be better off at home.'

'I would have bet on it.'

Before Nicola could make any comment, he pursued smoothly, 'So you finished college and had a white wedding... Then what?'

Unused to dissembling, she spoke the exact truth. 'I moved into Jeff's room.'

'Didn't you find being under your parents' roof somewhat...inhibiting?'

She had, more so than Jeff.

A little defensively, she explained, 'It wasn't how I would have chosen to do things. We'd both graduated with honours—Jeff in Design Engineering, me in Modern Languages and Business Studies—but neither of us had managed to get a job... In any case our parents, who had lived in rented accommodation all their lives, wanted us to stay with them until we could afford to start buying a place of our own, and Jeff was in agreement...

'I know that must sound a bit staid and unexciting...'

His voice almost angry, Dominic said, 'It sounds soul-destroying.'

Nicola flushed painfully.

Watching her colour rise, he apologised. 'I'm sorry, I shouldn't have made a remark like that.'

As lightly as possible, she said, 'That's all right. And it wasn't really so bad. At least Jeff and I were together...'

Then, wistfully, 'Though it would have been nice if we'd ever been able to move into a place of our own...'

'So you never succeeded in getting away?'

She shook her head. 'I'd managed to get an office job, but Jeff was unlucky. The company he'd joined made massive cutbacks, and he was one of the first to be made redundant, so we were still trying to save up when the accident happened.'

'Earlier you mentioned that after the accident you went to live with your friend Sandy?'

'Yes.'

'I'm surprised you didn't remain at home.'

'Our parents were killed in the same accident. The three of them were coming to pick me up from work when a lorry went out of control and hit them. We were all going on a family holiday.'

'So you were left with no one.'

'Sandy was very kind.'

'How did you cope with your freedom?'

She looked up startled. 'I suppose the answer's not too well. Though I never thought of it as *freedom*... It just seemed more like loneliness. I missed Jeff so much...'

'Having lived together for most of your lives, I suppose you were bound to. What was he like?'

'Very much like you.' She spoke without thinking.

The look in Dominic's eyes was swiftly veiled, yet she felt certain that he was far from pleased by the comparison.

Coolly, he said, 'Well, as you obviously loved him a great deal, I should feel flattered... Though I'm not convinced you know me well enough yet to compare us.'

'I—I meant in looks,' she stammered. 'Like you, he was tall, dark, and handsome...'

'A hackneyed phrase that can cover a multitude of sins,' Dominic observed mockingly. 'However, do go on.'

But as she described her late husband, visualising his face as she spoke and superimposing his features on the man sitting opposite, she knew her impression that they were alike was totally false.

The only similarity was the height and colouring.

Jeff had been over six foot, but compared to this man's broad chest and mature width of shoulder he had been... The thought that came to mind was *weedy*...

Feeling dreadfully disloyal, she pushed it away.

Both had hair that was a true black and wanted to curl, but while this man's was cut short and tamed Jeff's had been a boyish riot of tight ringlets.

He had still been boyish in many ways, his hands big-knuckled and bony, as though he hadn't yet grown into them, his face thin and sensitive-looking, with fine features and the air of a dreamer.

This man was anything but boyish. His hands were strong and well-shaped, with blunt fingers and neatly trimmed nails; his face was lean, with patrician features and an air of toughness and authority.

Jeff, by nature, had been kind and gentle and considerate.

Of Dominic's nature she knew nothing.

Yet looking at him now, and recalling the way he had adjusted her stole, she felt oddly certain that, like a lot of powerful men, he might well be tender and protective.

She missed that. The tenderness. The caring.

Watching her face, noting the wistful expression, and misinterpreting it, Dominic said, 'It's about time we changed the subject. You're starting to look sad, and talking about your husband can't be easy.'

'A short while ago, it wouldn't have been possible,' she admitted. 'But I think I'm finally coming to terms with his loss.'

That was the truth. Tonight, though there had been tricky bits, on the whole it had been relatively painless to talk about Jeff.

There were so many *happy* memories, and he would always have a very special place in her heart. But, as though a heavy load had been lifted, she no longer felt that crippling weight of grief she had carried for the past three years.

Watching her expression, Dominic said gravely, 'Welcome back to the world. What plans have you for the immediate future?'

'Short-term, I shall stay in Venice for a month or so. Make this holiday a new beginning. You see, I...'

His grey eyes were fixed on her face, intent, waiting.

On the point of telling him about John and her reason for travelling to Venice, she hesitated. Then, deciding she had done more than enough soul-baring for one night, changed her mind. 'I haven't taken a holiday since I joined Westlake, so I decided it was time I took a break.'

Their waiter appeared to ask if they wanted anything further and, after consulting Nicola, Dominic ordered coffee with cream for her, espresso for himself, and two brandies.

It arrived quite quickly, accompanied by a silver filigree plate of chocolates.

When the waiter had moved away on silent feet, Dominic asked, 'Have you ever been to Venice before?'

'No, though I've always wanted to. I've often visualised the warmth and colour, the wonderful old buildings, water everywhere, and crowds of people...'

'That about sums it up,' he said with a smile. 'Though the crowds are usually there only in the summer and at carnival time, and mostly in the touristy areas.'

'Then you don't find them a problem?'

'Not personally. There are many parts of Venice that hardly ever see a tourist—quiet backwaters, picturesque or decaying, depending on your point of view, where the ordinary Venetians live.'

'Have you lived there long?'

'All my life, apart from three years at Oxford and a year spent travelling. As I said, my father was from the States, but my mother's family have lived in Venice since the time of the Doges, when Italy was a great seafaring nation and one of the most prosperous settlements in Europe. Now, five hundred years past its heyday, Venice is still one of the most spectacular cities in the world.'

Noting that his voice held both enthusiasm and pride, she said, making it a statement rather than a question, 'And you like living there.'

'Yes, I do. For one thing it never becomes stale. There's always so much atmosphere, whether it's sunny, or rain-lashed, or there's a fog rolling in off the Adriatic. And in the evening Piazza San Marco is the perfect place for lovers. Something about the ambience makes couples of all ages sit and hold hands...'

The thought of sitting in Piazza San Marco holding hands with Dominic sent little shivers of excitement running through her.

Seeing that slight movement, he asked, 'Getting cold?' Before she could find her voice, he signalled the waiter, adding, 'I suppose it's time we were making a move. We've both got a fair drive tomorrow, and I could do with an early start.'

The bill paid, he rose to his feet and, with what she was beginning to recognise as his habitual courtesy, pulled out her chair.

Sorry that what had proved to be a magical evening was over, she allowed herself to be escorted back down the long, worn flight of steps, through the dining room and hall, and out into the flare-lit courtyard.

Dominic's car had been brought to the door, and, feeling

the chill of the night air, she was grateful that the hood was now up.

Cupping a hand beneath her bare elbow, making her pulses leap, Dominic settled her into her seat, then slid behind the wheel just as the Baron appeared and stood beneath the huge metal lantern to wave them off.

They both returned his wave, and a moment later they were through the archway and following the mountain road down to the valley.

Dominic drove with silent concentration as, their lights sweeping a path through the darkness, he negotiated the steep bends.

Nicola, very aware of his potent sex-appeal, thought only of him, and what tomorrow might hold when they reached Venice.

Feeling a thrill of expectation, she wondered whether he'd ask where she was staying, or suggest seeing her next morning before they each started their journey.

It would be lovely if he proposed having breakfast together...

She was still enjoying the glow of excitement and anticipation as they drew into the car park at the Bregenzerwald.

He helped her out and, a hand at her waist, accompanied her to the lift and pressed the button for the fifth floor.

When they reached her room she felt in her bag for the key and, having found it, fumbled to fit it into the lock.

She was starting to feel a little light-headed. Perhaps, as she wasn't used to drinking, she shouldn't have had a brandy with her coffee. But it was too late now.

'Allow me.' He took the key from her, and, having opened the door, handed it back with a smile.

'Thank you...'

She took a step into the room, and reached to put the key and her bag on the small table just inside the door. Then, with a sudden fear that he might just walk away, turned quickly to say, 'And thank you for a lovely evening. I've really enjoyed it.'

The sudden movement made her head spin, and, momentarily off balance, she swayed towards him and put her hands flat-palmed against his chest to steady herself. She could feel the warmth of his body through the fine lawn of his evening shirt.

Becoming aware that he had stiffened and was standing absolutely motionless, she backed away a step, saying huskily, 'I'm sorry.'

'There's really no need to be sorry... And I'm pleased you enjoyed the evening.'

Though the words were easy enough, there was a tautness about him, a look on his face that seemed to suggest a conflict of emotions, amongst them a touch of...censure?

It was gone in an instant, the smile back in place, convincing her that she must have imagined it.

A little awkwardly, she said, 'Well, goodnight.'

'Goodnight, Nicola.'

It was the first time he'd used her name.

Fascinated, she watched his mouth frame the syllables, and knew she wanted him to kiss her. *Needed* him to kiss her.

As though in answer to that unspoken need his hands closed around her upper arms and, drawing her towards him, he covered her mouth with his.

Though there was nothing diffident about it, his kiss was light, almost experimental, as though he was holding back to calculate her reaction before he decided exactly how to continue.

But once again her knees turned to water and her very bones seemed to melt, so that she was forced to lean against him for support.

His arms went around her, and as her lips parted helplessly beneath his he deepened the kiss.

It was like a brilliant flash of light, showing up both past and future, a revelation that was followed by a deep, black velvet darkness.

When he took her hand and led her into her room, closing the door behind them, she made not the slightest protest, conscious only of him and the need he had aroused.

Setting her back to the panels, one hand on the warmth of her nape, he bent to kiss her again while his free hand began to smooth over her slender figure: the small waist, the flare of her hip, the curve of her buttocks.

After a while the silk chiffon became an unwelcome barrier and, unzipping her dress, he eased it off her shoulders, allowing it to fall at her feet. Then his lips left hers to sensuously explore the line of her collarbone and the smooth skin of her shoulder.

When they reached the tender junction where neck and shoulder met, his kisses changed to little nibbling bites that made her stomach clench and her toes curl.

His mouth returning to hers, he unclipped her strapless bra and, cupping one of her small, firm breasts, brushed his thumb over the nipple.

While she was still struggling to cope with the sensations he was provoking, he bent his head and, having laved the other erect nipple, took it into his mouth and suckled sweetly.

She was suddenly into sensual overload, the pleasure so intense that she gave a little moan and, running her fingers into his dark hair, held his head away from her breast.

A moment later she was swept up in his arms and carried to the bed. The only light was from the street outside, but in the gloom she saw the gleam of his eyes as he laid her carefully on top of the covers and sat down beside her to take off what remained of her clothing.

CHAPTER THREE

IT WAS so long since she had been tenderly held and made love to, so long since she had felt the warmth of being needed, that far from objecting, half choked by eagerness, she would have helped him had it been necessary.

But his hands were both gentle and deft, and though he didn't linger, neither did he show the slightest sign of haste.

When she was totally naked, he said with a kind of urgency, 'Let your hair loose,' and, as she lifted her hands to obey, began to strip off his own clothes.

As her hair came tumbling around her shoulders, he sat on the edge of the bed and, running his fingers into the thick silky mass, began to kiss her again.

When he finally joined her on the bed, her arms were ready to welcome him, but stretching out beside her, he propped himself on one elbow, taking time to pleasure her, while he enjoyed a body that, he told her softly, was the loveliest he'd ever seen.

As he stroked and touched and tasted, she clenched and unclenched her hands, lost and mindless, caught up and engulfed by the kind of suffocating hunger and excitement she had never experienced in her life before.

Everything he was doing now only served to suck her deeper into a black and spinning whirlpool of desire, and by the time he made them one she was a quivering mass of sensations and desperate for the release that only he could provide.

Nicola floated to the surface to find it was broad daylight. The curtains hadn't been pulled to, and the early-morning sun was pouring in.

For a little while she lay half-asleep and half-awake, gazing up at the white ceiling, where a reflected sunbeam danced. She felt relaxed and contented in a way she hadn't felt for years.

She was trying lazily to brush aside the last clinging cobwebs of sleep to find the reason for her euphoria when, as though in answer, her mind was filled with thoughts of Dominic.

Memories of his dark, handsome face and the infinite rapture and delight he had given her came flooding back.

Her heart filled to overflowing, she turned her head.

She was alone in the bed, and his clothes had vanished. Presumably, for the look of the thing, he had gone back to his own room. But just the imprint of his head in the pillow beside her, and the recollection of his lovemaking, was as warming as the sun.

For so long the world had seemed a cold and lonely place. No love, no warmth, no joy. She had denied and suppressed all her natural needs, keeping her longings and emotions packed away in ice while life went on around her.

Now, as though to make up for the blows it had inflicted, fate had offered her a second chance of happiness.

A chance she had snatched at in a way that was not only completely unlike her but which, in her right mind, she would have regarded as wild and irresponsible.

In the normal course of events a new relationship would have moved forward at a steadier rate—getting to know one another, becoming friends, and then finally lovers.

But somehow they had skipped the first two stages. All she knew about Dominic was what she had discovered in a single afternoon and evening. That he was an excellent companion, intelligent and charming, with a dry humour and a curiously old-fashioned sense of chivalry.

She had no real idea what made him tick as a person.

After all her foster mother's dire warnings she had gone to bed with a man she had only just met; a man who was a virtual stranger. A departure from the norm that she was forced to admit was dangerous to the point of lunacy.

Though she couldn't regret a moment of it, she found herself wondering what on earth had made her behave so recklessly.

Too much alcohol had undoubtedly contributed, by putting her on a high and lulling her inhibitions. But if she was truthful, she knew the alcohol wasn't to blame.

She had found Dominic irresistibly attractive from the word go, and the whole magical evening—the drive, the *schloss*, the ambience, the good food and wonderful scenery—had all played a part.

A scene set for seduction.

Except that she couldn't blame him. She had *wanted* what happened. Probably more than he had, she admitted, recalling his first reaction to what she now realised uneasily must have appeared to be a come-on.

Perhaps if she explained to him that she wasn't used to drinking…? Or would it be better to say nothing? She didn't want him to feel guilty in any way, or think that she was trying to put the blame on him.

But why should there be any suggestion of guilt or blame? He certainly hadn't pressured her. She had been a willing partner…

And it had been *wonderful*. She sighed. As well as being a skilful lover, he had been generous and considerate and, remembering the controlled passion of his lovemaking, her heart began to beat faster.

Jeff's lovemaking had been kind and tender, warm and caring, but she hadn't realised until last night how much it had lacked passion. Or skill.

How much she had missed.

Her main pleasure, quite often her *only* pleasure, had been lying in his arms afterwards, happy that he was satisfied and contented.

Maybe it had been her own fault. Perhaps she had felt too inhibited to let go and enjoy the side of marriage that she was convinced her foster mother had secretly regarded as 'not quite nice'.

Things might have been different if she and Jeff had managed to get away—*get away*...she was using Dominic's words—but it was no use thinking about what might have been. That part of her life was over. Fate had written *finis* to it.

Now, at last, with John's encouragement, and having met Dominic, she was moving forward into a new, exciting, and hopefully much happier phase.

Thinking of Dominic, and recalling how he had mentioned getting an early start, she glanced at her watch. It was gone eight-thirty. He was probably waiting for her in the breakfast room, wondering where on earth she'd got to.

Pushing aside the light covers, she scrambled out of bed. Her discarded clothes, she noticed, had been picked up and placed neatly over a chair.

As soon as she had cleaned her teeth and showered she dressed in a light two-piece and flat shoes that she judged would be easy to drive in, and hastily repacked her cases.

Standing in front of the mirror, she saw a strange young woman with a smile hanging on her lips. A happy and excited woman, who had a glowing, heart-shaped face and sparkling green eyes.

With a feeling of *joie de vivre*, she smiled back.

She was halfway through taking her hair up into its usual neat coil when, recalling the way Dominic had run his fingers through it, her heart picked up speed and her hands started to tremble.

Telling herself not to be foolish, she finished pushing in

the pins and, leaving her luggage where it was, hurried to the lift, eager as a young Juliet.

The breakfast room faced east and was light and airy, with a crescent-shaped counter that held fruit and cereals, rolls and croissants, ham, cheeses, and various preserves.

Three or four tables were occupied, and an elderly couple were standing by the buffet debating in English whether to have rolls or croissants. Dominic was nowhere to be seen.

So she was first down after all. Making up her mind to tease him about it, Nicola helped herself to fruit juice and a croissant, and sat down at a table for two. When a waiter appeared, she asked for coffee.

By the time she had eaten her croissant and drunk two cups of coffee, there was still no sign of him.

She went back upstairs and tapped at his door.

There was no answer.

Thinking he might possibly be in the shower, she knocked harder.

Still no answer.

As she stood hesitating in the corridor, wondering what to do for the best, a chambermaid appeared pushing a trolley loaded with fresh bedlinen.

With a curious glance at Nicola, she opened the door of number 54 with a master-key.

'The man who has this room…' Nicola said carefully, 'I was hoping to speak to him.'

'He has gone, *fräulein*. The room is empty.'

'Oh.' Somehow they must have missed each other. Possibly he was at the desk paying his bill.

Letting herself back into her own room, Nicola gathered together her luggage and took the lift down to the foyer.

There were quite a few people there, including the bullet-headed man she had seen the previous day, but no Dominic.

She paid her own bill and made her way down to the car park. Having stowed everything in the boot, she locked the car and crossed to the far bay where Dominic's white car had been parked.

It was no longer there.

The realisation was like a blow in the solar plexus.

Surely he hadn't just gone without a word?

Hurrying back to the desk, she gave her name to the desk clerk and asked, 'Did anyone leave a note for me?'

A white envelope with the hotel logo was produced. 'My apologies, *fräulein*. It should have been given to you when you checked out, but it was overlooked.'

Sinking into one of the maroon leather chairs, she tore it open.

Written on a sheet of hotel notepaper, in a clear, positive hand, it said simply:

> A business commitment meant I had to make an early start, and you were sleeping so peacefully when I left that it seemed a shame to disturb you.
>
> Have a good journey. I'm looking forward to seeing you in Venice.
>
> Dominic

I'm looking forward to seeing you in Venice...

But he'd never asked where she was staying, nor had he told her where he lived.

In answer to his questions she had poured out her life story, while he had told her virtually nothing about himself. All she really knew was that he was a businessman who lived in Venice.

Venice was a big city. A lot of people lived there.

As Nicola sat and stared blankly at the sheet of paper, it was borne upon her that he had opted out. If he really *had* wanted to see her in Venice he would have given her a phone number, told her where to contact him.

Her feeling of excitement vanished as if it had never been, and she bit her lip until she tasted the warm, sticky saltiness of blood.

After being cautious, inhibited even, all her life, she had thrown aside all restraints and behaved totally out of character.

Like the worst kind of fool, she had regarded their night together as *special*, the start of a wonderful relationship. But as far as he was concerned it had been just been a one-night stand.

If he had seemed caring and tender, it hadn't meant he *cared* in the slightest. Only that he was a good lover. To him she had merely been a woman who was willing, not to say eager, to go to bed with him.

He must be used to women throwing themselves at him. With his looks and charisma it probably happened a lot.

Recalling his momentary hesitation before he had kissed her, the look on his face that she was now convinced *had* been censure, she was filled with a sense of shame and humiliation. She had thrown herself at a man who must have felt little but contempt for her.

He might even be married.

She hadn't asked, and he hadn't mentioned it. But then, if he *was* cheating on his wife he wouldn't want to publicise the fact.

Thinking about it logically, as he was half Italian and living in Italy, he was almost certainly married, and probably had a family. Italian males tended to marry at a younger age than their English counterparts, and he must be somewhere in the region of thirty.

Feeling as if her heart had shrivelled inside her, she was about to drop the note into the nearest litter bin, when at the last instant she changed her mind and thrust it into her bag.

He had written it, it was the only tangible link, and somehow, although she knew she was acting like a weak fool, she couldn't bring herself to simply throw it away.

It was a beautiful day, with golden sunshine, a sky the colour of cornflowers, and a few white cotton wool clouds. But all the pleasant anticipation of the journey had gone as, heavy-hearted and bitterly ashamed of her actions, she drove out of Innsbruck and headed south for Italy.

Telling herself firmly that it was no use crying over what couldn't be altered, she tried hard to put Dominic Loredan and everything that had happened right out of her mind.

It was next door to impossible.

His strong, handsome face haunted her, and time after time she had to struggle to banish memories of his voice and his smile, his experienced hands and the touch of his mouth on hers.

However, by dint of concentrating on her driving and the magnificent mountain scenery, she managed to go for quite long periods without thinking of him, and she found the journey over the Brenner Pass both picturesque and interesting.

After a while she decided to have some music, and reaching for one of the tapes she had brought with her for the journey, slotted it in.

After a moment the first vibrant notes of a Rachmaninov piano concerto filled the car.

She hadn't been able to listen to that kind of music whilst living at home. Her foster parents had disapproved of Rachmaninov, thinking him too unrestrained.

Now, listening to the beautiful, passionate music, Nicola's thoughts turned once again to Dominic, and the night they had spent together.

She had awakened just as dawn was breaking to find herself held in the crook of his arm, her head on his shoulder, her body half supported by his.

He had been lying quietly on his back, his eyes open, his jaw covered in a dark stubble that made him look even more masculine and sexy.

Overjoyed that he was still with her, she had nestled against him.

His arm tightening in response, he had begun to fondle her breast, making her heart beat faster with pleasure and anticipation.

She had touched him then, tracing his ribcage, the muscles beneath the smooth, tanned skin, the line of his collarbone and his small, taut nipples.

Hearing his slight intake of breath, and wondering if her touch was giving him a fraction of the pleasure his was giving her, greatly daring, she had allowed her hand to wander downwards past the trim waist and over the flat stomach.

Turning his head so that his lips were brushing her hair, he had murmured, 'If you go on doing that you'll be in trouble.'

She, who had never in her life played this kind of lovers' game, had found herself asking provocatively, 'What kind of trouble?'

'Big trouble.'

'I think I can stand it.'

The words had ended in a gasp as he'd rolled her over, pinning her beneath him. 'Do you now?' he'd asked silkily.

Thinking of what had happened next, the pleasure they had shared before falling asleep again, made heat run through her. But rather than the heat of passion it was a burning humiliation.

Having stopped at a convenient roadside restaurant for lunch, it was late afternoon by the time she reached Venice and drove over the three-and-a-half kilometre Ponte della Liberta.

The built-up coastal strip had been flat and relatively uninteresting, and, apart from the bridge itself, this approach to the city seemed to be little better.

Then all at once its domes and spires began to appear, strangely beautiful and insubstantial as any mirage in the shimmering air.

Piazzale Roma, on the other hand, was as prosaic as any large square that was also a bus terminus. Edged by stalls selling cold drinks and hot dogs, chilled water melon and thin white slices of fresh coconut, it was hot and crowded and dusty, full of engine noise and diesel fumes, and the smell of fried onions.

No traffic went beyond the *piazzale*. All road vehicles were left either in the blocks of private garages or in the huge public car parks.

Unsure quite where to go, Nicola drew to a halt and hesitated. A boy of perhaps eleven or twelve, wearing a torn T-shirt and sneakers, came up to the car and said through the open window. 'You English? On holiday?'

'Yes,' she answered a shade cautiously.

'I look after case while you park car. Then I show you where to get *vaporetto*.'

Dared she chance leaving her luggage with this brown-skinned urchin? Or would he disappear with it while her back was turned?

To give herself a moment to think, she remarked, 'You speak good English.'

'I learn from my cousin's wife. She 'as live in America long time. You put case here—' he indicated a flagged area by some stone steps '—I guard till you come back.'

Everything of real value was in her overnight case, and, used to travelling light, in this temperature it would be a boon if she *could* leave the big suitcase.

Seeing her waver, he urged, 'You OK... I no steal.'

'What's your name?'

'Carlo Foscari.'

He gave his name without hesitation. Making up her mind, Nicola opened the car door and started to get out. Her skirt rode up a little, and as she smoothed it over her knees she saw a short, thick-set man, with blue jowls and black hair, staring at her intently.

Recalling what Sandy had said about Italian males, she pretended not to notice.

Sun beat down from a cloudless sky and heat struck through the thin soles of her sandals as she lifted out her big suitcase and set it down in the gritty dust. When she looked up, the man who had been staring at her had vanished.

Opening her bag, she took out enough *lira* notes to hopefully make the ready cash more useful than a case full of clothing, and tore them in two. Giving one half to the boy, she put the other half back in her bag.

To her surprise, he grinned as he thrust them into the pocket of his frayed khaki shorts. 'I tell you no trust me.'

Grinning back, she asked in Italian, 'Would you, in my place?'

He gave her a look of respect. 'You speak Italian good, *signorina*...?'

'Whitney,' she supplied.

'Whitney...' He had a fair shot at it. 'But I practise my English...' Waving a grubby paw, he instructed, 'Go that way to long stay car park. I wait here.'

When she returned with a ticket and her overnight case, he gave her a cheeky grin. 'See! I no steal.'

'I should hope not,' she told him severely.

'This way,' he said importantly, and seized the big suitcase.

'You'd better let me have that,' she objected. 'It's too heavy for you.'

'Then I take small one.'

She shook her head.

'OK… I get help.' Putting two fingers to his lips, he gave a piercing whistle. 'Mario will come.'

Mario, a handsome young man with brown wavy hair and soulful dark eyes, appeared from nowhere.

'My brother,' Carlo explained briefly.

Nicola found herself escorted, one on either side, down the flight of stone steps to the Grand Canal and the landing-stage for the *vaporetti*.

Venice's main thoroughfare was wider than she had imagined, the sparkling water teeming with craft of all shapes and sizes, barges, motorboats, gondolas.

'See, it come.' Carlo sounded personally responsible for the arrival of the crowded water-bus which was approaching the landing stage.

Taking the torn *lira* notes from her bag, Nicola handed them to him. '*Grazie*, Carlo.'

Mario was appreciably older, eighteen or nineteen, she guessed, and a great deal better dressed. She was wondering whether to tip him when, as though reading her difficulty, he smiled at her, his teeth very white, and said, 'It was my pleasure, *signorina*.'

Glad that she hadn't hurt his feelings, she said, '*Grazie*, Mario,' and with a single smile made him forget the girl he'd been planning to take out that evening.

'Where you stay?' Carlo enquired.

'Hotel Lunga. Campo Dolini.'

'I know. You get *biglietto* to San Sebastian. Go down Calle Dolini.'

The *vaporetto* drew into the landing stage and bumped heavily a couple of times, before being moored. As they were practically swamped by the crowds streaming off it,

Carlo suggested hopefully, 'Tonight you wish for guide to see Venice?'

'*Non, grazie.*'

Looking disappointed, he persisted, 'Tomorrow morning, maybe?'

'No, thank you, Carlo.'

As she was carried forward by the surge of people waiting to get on the boat, he called, '*Ciao*, Signorina Whitney.'

By the time she had managed to struggle aboard and find a few feet of space to put her cases down, both Carlo and Mario had been swallowed up by the crowd.

As soon as the *vaporetto* began to move Nicola enjoyed the cooling breeze standing by the rail. Sun glinted on the pale blue-green water, and the light was so dazzling that she felt in her bag for her sunglasses.

The Grand Canal, picturesque and colourful in pastel hues, like a Canaletto painting come to life, was lined on either side with pale marble *palazzos*, baroque and rococo churches, and fine old buildings.

Some of them appeared to be sadly neglected, their crumbling steps and low-lying frontage blotched with patches of black, slimy seaweed. Yet, hauntingly beautiful even in their decay, they still held echoes of a former glory.

Though he hadn't been Italian by birth, this had been John's city.

It was also Dominic's…

The recollection brought a sudden lump to her throat, and she was still endeavouring to banish thoughts of Dominic from her mind when the boat reached San Sebastian.

Gathering up her luggage, she disembarked along with a small crowd of people, some locals, some obviously tourists.

Though the air seemed still and heavy, occasional little gusts of hot wind sprang up from nowhere, rattling the awnings of closed shops and swirling the dust.

Calle Dolini was a narrow street to the left, and she

walked along the shady side, putting the big case down
briefly from time to time.

Away from the main *fondamenta*, and in the heat of the
day, there was no one about apart from one man who was
quite a distance behind her. Obviously in no hurry, he never
caught her up, despite the stops.

When she finally emerged into Campo Dolini, she found
that it was a quiet, dusty square surrounded by buildings
with closed shutters.

What was obviously the rear entrance to Hotel Lunga
looked distinctly unpromising, with crumbling stucco, narrow, shuttered windows and peeling doors.

Inside, however, it was positively luxurious, with polished marble floors and crystal chandeliers.

Standing by the desk in the foyer, she could see that the
hotel's main entrance fronted on to a canal which ran par-
allel to the end of the *campo*. Steps led down to a private
landing stage for the guests arriving by water-taxi.

Which of course, Nicola realised belatedly, *she* should
have done. Though the *vaporetto* had been an experience
she wouldn't have missed.

When she had checked in, she took the lift up to her third-
floor room. It was cool and dim and spacious, with terrazzo
flooring and the absolute minimum of light, modern furniture.

The windows were open wide, but the slatted shutters had
been closed to keep out the sun. Opening them a few inches,
she found herself looking over the *campo*, two-thirds of
which lay in bright sunlight, the other third in shade.

As she stood by the window she noticed a man standing
in the deep shadows at the far end of the square. He was of
similar height and build to the man who had stared at her
in the Piazzale Roma.

Her hand on the wooden shutter, she leaned forward to

try and get a better view. Squeaking a protest, it suddenly swung wide.

When she regained her balance and looked again, there wasn't a soul to be seen.

A glance in the *en suite* bathroom showed it was well-appointed, and, hot and sticky after her walk in the sun, she decided that her first priority was to shower and change.

As she stood beneath the warm water, smoothing shower-gel over her slick body, she remembered how Dominic's hand had explored her curves... How he had cupped her breast and rubbed his thumb lightly over the nipple, sending needle-sharp darts of pleasure through her... The way his tongue had laved the other nipple before his mouth had closed over it...

Shuddering, she tried to push the erotic imagery away, but already her whole body was growing alive and eager, every nerve-ending tightening in response...

With a sudden savage movement, she turned the water to cold, and gasped as the shock hit her.

Dried and duly sprayed with *Adventure*, the body mist Sandy had insisted on giving her as a 'seeing Venice present', she opened her case and found fresh undies and a silky sage-green dress with a loose matching jacket.

Deciding to abandon the rest of her unpacking until later, she slipped her slender feet into a comfortable pair of strappy sandals with a small heel, and smoothed on some sunscreen.

Then, having helped herself to a complimentary Pianta di Venezia, on an impulse she dropped the keys to Ca' Malvasia into her bag before setting off to explore.

Leaving the hotel by the main entrance, she paused on the sunlit pavement for a moment to study the map. Piazza San Marco, the hub of the city, was on the lagoon, and easy to find...

Abruptly, Dominic's tough, attractive face filled her mind, and the notion that he was almost certainly here, in Venice, maybe not too far away, was a bittersweet one.

Feeling as though her heart was being constricted by iron bands, she thought, If only things could have been different. He was the kind of man she would have been happy to spend the rest of her life with.

Oh, don't be such a fool! she berated herself crossly. How could she possibly think such a stupid thing? She didn't *know* him. And if she was right in her assumption that he was married, would she seriously want a man who could so casually cheat on his wife?

Pushing away memories of Dominic for perhaps the hundredth time that day, Nicola returned to the map to try and locate the house she could still hardly believe was hers.

Signor Mancini had told her that Ca' Malvasia was situated on Campo dei Cavalli, and quite close to the Grand Canal. He had added that the Rio dei Cavalli ran behind the property, so it was also accessible from the water.

Knowing that the Rio dei Cavalli should be easier to find than a square, she followed the curve of the Grand Canal scanning both banks... Yes, there it was—and, close by, the *campo*.

First thing in the morning she had an appointment with Signor Mancini, to be shown over Ca' Malvasia, but with a sudden surge of impatience, she decided that if she could find it now she would take a look at the outside at least.

She walked down the *fondamenta* and crossed a humpbacked bridge with ornate wrought-iron railings, and headed west.

The early-evening light was low and golden, scaling the crumbling stone and brickwork and slanting across water that, in the back canals, was the oily, opaque green of pea soup.

It didn't take her long to realise how easy it would be to

get lost in Venice. Away from the centre it was a labyrinth of narrow streets, the names of which were set high on the corners of buildings. Some were written in Venetian dialect, which made them more difficult to decipher.

It would no doubt have been a great deal simpler to have gone back to the Grand Canal and followed that, but she wanted to see the parts of Venice that tourists rarely, if ever, visited.

The everyday Venice that John had been familiar with. The Venice that Dominic knew and loved.

CHAPTER FOUR

MOST of the houses she passed en route had shuttered windows that gave them a blind, empty look. But the rattle of crockery and the sound of television suggested that many families were home and about to sit down to an early-evening meal.

Because of the network of waterways it was impossible to take a straight line so, zigzagging, crossing innumerable small bridges, she finally found an alleyway that led her to her goal.

At first glance, Campo dei Cavalli looked to be merely a quiet backwater with a few shady trees, but a handsome marble fountain in the centre, its four long-maned horses galloping through sea spray, spoke of more illustrious days.

Dominated on one side by a huge church, the *campo* appeared to be still and deserted, the only movement a swirling dust devil whipped up by a sudden gust of wind.

But as Nicola glanced around she saw a man with a mobile phone to his ear just disappearing into one of the alleyways that quartered the square. In such a setting it seemed incongruous.

Backing on to the Rio dei Cavalli were several old and handsome *palazzos*, whose intricate, lace-like façades and arched windows gave them a Gothic look.

Signor Mancini had mentioned that Ca' Malvasia backed on to the water, but surely none of those grand palaces could be the house she was looking for? Perhaps she had misunderstood, and it wasn't actually on the *campo*?

As she stood uncertainly, an old lady dressed all in black, her head covered by a lacy shawl, left the church by a small door set into the massive main doors and headed in her direction.

'*Scusi, signora,*' Nicola began politely, 'but can you help me? I'm looking for Ca' Malvasia.'

'It adjoins Palazzo dei Cavalli.'

Nicola could see no break in the façade of the palace the wizened hand was pointing at.

Seeing that blank look, the old lady, whose face was brown and wrinkled as a walnut, broke into a toothless grin. 'At one time Ca' Malvasia was part of the *palazzo*. There is the door.'

To the right of the *palazzo*'s imposing entrance, a flight of curved steps ran up to a black, studded door with a lantern hanging above it, and a series of long narrow windows on either side.

'*Grazie, signora. Buona sera.*'

'*Buona sera.*'

Nodding affably, the old lady went on her way, while Nicola tilted back her head and shaded her eyes to peer up at the house that was now hers.

Four storeys high, the top two storeys with balconies, Ca' Malvasia looked much bigger and far grander than she had ever imagined. There were no windows on the lowest floor, which suggested it was a boat-house, and all the upper windows appeared to be tightly shuttered.

She climbed the steps, and after feeling in her bag for the keys tried the largest in the lock. It moved quite easily.

Grasping the ornate iron ring, she pushed open the heavy door and took a few steps inside. After the heat and glare of the Campo dei Cavalli it was pleasantly cool and dark.

The air smelled slightly musty and vault-like, which wasn't surprising if the house had been closed up for years.

When her eyes had adjusted to the gloom, Nicola found she was standing in a marble-floored hall, with a beautiful central staircase.

The slatted shutters let in just enough light to enable her to make out several closed doors on either side.

Having got this far, it seemed a shame not to take a quick look at the rest of the house... Though the last thing she wanted to do was hurt Signor Mancini's feelings by preempting him...

But so long as she didn't open the shutters or disturb anything he need never know she'd already been here.

Her mind made up, she felt a little thrill of excitement.

There were electricity switches on the wall by the door, and without much hope she tried a couple.

Nothing happened.

Oh, well, she could at least get *some* idea of the layout.

Leaving the front door partly open, she crossed the hall and began to peer into the various rooms. Even in the shuttered dimness she could tell they were magnificent, with painted ceilings and antique furnishings.

At the far end, an arched door gave on to a wide stone corridor and what she guessed had once been kitchens and servants' quarters. She could just make out that a flight of worn stone steps disappeared upwards into blackness.

Returning to the hall, where a brilliant lozenge of light from the open door lay on the pale marble floor, she climbed the elegant staircase which led up to a gallery with four long, shuttered windows.

She had just reached the top step when a sudden loud thud made her jump. It was still echoing hollowly when she spun round to see that the slanting oblong of light had disappeared.

The front door was closed.

Perhaps one of those freak gusts of wind had swirled in? Or maybe the door's own weight had caused it to gradually swing shut?

Suddenly uneasy for no good reason, she hesitated, wondering whether to go down and open it again.

But that small amount of light would make no difference to the upper floor she was about to explore, and perhaps the door would be safer closed?

There must be a lot of valuable things in the house, and she had no idea of the opportunist crime rate in Venice.

The echoes had died away, and once more absolute silence reigned. For a few moments she stood, listening to that absence of sound until she fancied she could hear her own breathing and heartbeat.

Then, collecting herself, she moved to open the nearest door. The rooms on this floor, though large and grand by ordinary standards, were obviously the ones John and his wife had lived in.

Through the gloom she could make out that all the decors were light, and the furnishings relatively modern, though the doors, like the doors on the lower floor, had heavy metal handles and large iron locks, some with keys.

Everywhere had the dusty, deadened aspect that places seemed to acquire when they'd stood empty for a long time.

A stone archway beckoned and, wondering where the corridor led to, Nicola set off cautiously down it. Away from the faint light that filtered through the gallery's shuttered windows, it was even darker, and she moved with one hand on the nearest wall.

Above the faint rasping noise it made, she suddenly became aware of another stealthy sound.

A chill running through her, she stopped and turned, peering into the darkness, holding her breath while she listened.

There it was again, the merest brush of a footfall. The tiny hairs on the back of her neck rose.

Though in the close confines of the stone corridor the sound seemed to whisper around her, making it impossible to tell exactly where it was coming from, she knew someone must be following her.

Someone who was closing in on her.

Someone who was blocking her escape route.

Her breath caught in her throat, her heart pounding, she realised with sudden clarity that her only option was to go on. When she reached a door, it might be possible to lock it while she opened the window and called for help.

Feeling as though she was caught up in some awful nightmare, she turned and forced her shaking legs to carry her forward.

She had taken only a few hurried steps when a dark shape detached itself from the surrounding darkness and loomed up in front of her.

Far from following her, whoever it was had been lying in wait for her.

A strangled scream was torn from her throat, and, gripped by blind panic, she turned to flee back the way she had come.

'Nicola, stop!' a voice cried sharply. 'If you try to run in the dark you'll only hurt yourself.'

Before she could heed the warning her ankle turned under her, and she went sprawling, her head hitting the wall with a sharp crack.

When she regained consciousness she was lying full length on a couch, minus her jacket and shoes. A bearded, middle-aged man was bending over her, examining her left temple.

Straightening up, and addressing someone she couldn't see, he observed in Italian, 'Luckily it seems to have been just a glancing blow.'

Then, with the air of a conjuror producing a rabbit from a hat, he produced a pencil torch from a black briefcase and shone a fine beam into first one eye and then the other.

After due consideration he gave his verdict briskly. 'There is no evidence of any concussion, I'm pleased to say. Now, you mentioned the possibility of a sprained ankle...'

He bent to examine her left ankle, which was starting to swell.

She winced as his fingers pressed and prodded. 'Yes, a slight sprain. There may be a little pain and stiffness, some further swelling, perhaps, but again no long-lasting damage.'

Producing a small canister, he sprayed the affected area. It felt icy cold, and seemed to tighten around her ankle like an invisible tourniquet.

Replacing the torch and the canister, he said, 'I'll leave some painkillers. The patient should take two immediately, and then as necessary. If there should be any signs of nausea or blurred vision, perhaps you'll let me know as soon as possible?'

'Of course. Many thanks for coming so quickly, Doctor. Stefano will show you out.'

Though she couldn't see the second man, and had never heard him speak in Italian before, she would have recognised that voice anywhere.

Had recognised it, when it was too late and she was already embarked on her headlong flight.

'How are you feeling?' Casually dressed in light trousers and a sports shirt, his dark, attractive face serious, Dominic came to stand by her side.

'I'm fine,' she answered, trying to struggle into a sitting position.

The sudden movement sent her head spinning and she closed her eyes. No, she thought dazedly, the whole thing had to be just a vivid dream. It couldn't possibly be Dominic.

Opening them again, she saw that it was.

'I don't understand,' she said weakly, as he carefully helped her up and put a cushion behind her back.

'What don't you understand?'

'Anything... Where I am. What I'm doing here. Why *you're* here...'

'You're at the Palazzo dei Cavalli, and I'm here because this is where I live.'

Ironically, he added, 'In case you haven't realised yet, we're neighbours. I brought you back here after you passed out.'

She put a hand to her throbbing temple. 'But what were you doing in Ca' Malvasia?'

When he didn't immediately answer, she added, 'And how do you know we're neighbours?'

Coolly, he said, 'It would make sense to leave the rest of the questions until later. You've had quite a nasty shock, as well as a bump on the head. I'll get my housekeeper to bring you a cup of tea and a couple of the painkillers Dr Castello left. When you've had those, I suggest that you keep your feet up until I've finished my business. Then if you feel well enough we'll do some serious talking.'

Before she could make any attempt to argue he turned away, and a moment later the carved oak door closed quietly behind him.

Feeling as if she needed to pinch herself, Nicola looked around her for the first time. She was in a handsome, well-proportioned room which, in spite of the half-closed shutters, gave the impression of being light and airy.

It was furnished as a living room-cum-study, with an eclectic mix of old and new, and, despite its palatial grandeur, looked comfortable and lived-in.

But what was Dominic Loredan doing living here?

Well, why not? She made an attempt to rationalise things. He had said he lived in Venice. The fact that he lived in a *palazzo* wasn't too strange. Because of its former wealth and historical grandeur, a lot of people in Venice must live in a *palazzo*.

What was strange was that out of the whole sprawling

city he should live next door to the house that had been John's and was now hers.

Coincidences did happen, and truth, it had often been said, was stranger than fiction. But surely this was too fantastic for words? An unbelievable coincidence…?

Another thought struck her. Though it had been dark in the passage at Ca' Malvasia, and Dominic couldn't possibly have seen her face, he had known who she was. He had called, 'Nicola, stop!'…

Her musings were interrupted by an elderly woman dressed all in black, carrying a tray of tea.

Setting it down on a low table near the couch, she indicated two white tablets on a small saucer, and said in halting English, 'Signor Dominic say to take.'

'Thank you…?'

'Maria,' she supplied.

'*Grazie*, Maria.'

'You speak Italian?'

'*Si.*'

A look of relief spreading over her broad face, the housekeeper said in her own language, 'Dominic asked me to tell you that he will be with you in about an hour…' Picking up the silver teapot, she filled a porcelain cup, before going on, 'He said to remind you that when you have drunk your tea, he would like you to lie down and rest quietly.'

Though politely phrased, Maria obviously regarded her master's request as an order.

'*Grazie,*' Nicola said.

'Is there anything further you need, *signorina*?'

'*Non, grazie*, Maria.'

When the housekeeper had gone, Nicola sipped her tea and swallowed the tablets. Young and resilient, she was already starting to feel much better but, unwilling to rock the boat, she decided to rest as Dominic had asked.

Trying to ignore the questions that buzzed in her head

like a swarm of bees, she stretched out full length once more and closed her eyes...

With so much on her mind she hadn't expected to sleep, but when she opened them again Dominic was sitting on the edge of the couch, one arm resting against the back, looking down at her.

Though she was unable to decipher the expression on his face, something about his posture convinced her he had been there for a little while, watching her.

The idea was an oddly disturbing one. It made her feel vulnerable, at a disadvantage.

He had changed into a white shirt and a well-cut evening jacket, and, freshly shaved, his black hair still damp from the shower, he looked fit and vital and devastatingly handsome.

His grey eyes studying her face, he asked, 'How are you feeling now?'

'Fine.'

'If I remember, you told me that earlier, when it was patently a lie.'

'Well, now it's the truth.'

'Hungry?'

'Starving.'

'I find that reassuring. Are you happy to eat here...?'

She hesitated. The last thing she wanted to do was find herself eating with his wife...

'Or would you prefer to go out, if the ankle will allow it?'

'Are you married?' The words were spoken before she could prevent them and, horrified by the bluntness of the question, she stammered, 'I—I mean if you have a wife and family to consider...'

His smile faintly mocking, he said flatly, 'I'm not married. The only family I have is a younger brother, David, who is away on business until tomorrow.'

She felt almost faint with relief.

'So which is it to be?'

'Out, please,' she said breathlessly.

No matter what, it would be wonderful to get her first sight of Venice by night with Dominic at her side.

'Are you sure that both your head and ankle will stand it?'

'Quite sure.'

All at once she was filled with hope and vitality. Though there were a lot of questions still to be answered, none of them really mattered.

Dominic was not only unmarried, but somehow he had contrived to find her again, and the bitter disappointment of the morning had vanished as if it had never been.

'Let me see how steady on your feet you are.'

Holding out a hand, he helped her up, and waited with his palm cupped lightly beneath her bare elbow. Something like an electric current sensitised her skin, and she felt a shiver run through her.

Head bent, so he wouldn't see how much his touch affected her, she stood as instructed, ignoring the slight twinge of pain that shot through her injured ankle.

'No discomfort?'

'None,' she lied.

'Then I think you'll do. There's a bathroom through here if you'd like to freshen up before we start?'

'Oh, yes, please,' she said gratefully.

Her jacket, sandals and handbag had been placed on a chair and, gathering them up, she followed him.

He opened a door to the left and showed her into a room that Sandy would have unhesitatingly described as 'big enough to hold a ball in'.

It was luxuriously equipped and, suddenly feeling dusty and dishevelled, she asked, 'Do you think I could have a quick shower?'

'Of course.' Straight-faced, he added, 'If you need any help just give me a shout.'

When he had gone, closing the door behind him, she turned on the water and, after stripping off, stepped into the shower stall.

Careful not to get her hair wet, she showered as swiftly as possible, dried herself on a fluffy towel and, feeling greatly refreshed, pulled on her clothes, pleased to see that her fall hadn't marked them.

It took less than a minute to comb out her thick blonde hair and recoil it, and she was ready.

At her entrance, Dominic tossed aside the paper he'd been reading and rose to his feet. 'A woman of her word, I see,' he congratulated her. 'Feeling better?'

'Much better.'

'Then let's go. But to be on the safe side I'd like you to stay off your feet as much as possible.'

Nicola had presumed they would walk, but, a hand at her waist, he escorted her across a magnificent hall, through a door, and down a flight of marble steps.

Favouring her sprained ankle, she descended with care into what was obviously the main boat-house. There were several craft moored there, amongst them two sleek motor-boats.

From the landing stage another few steps led down to where the nearest motorboat, which was tied to an iron ring set in the stonework, was bobbing about on the blue-green water.

He helped her in, and when she was settled, took the controls and headed up the Rio dei Cavalli to the Grand Canal.

Feeling as though she was in a dream, she studied his strong profile, the way the breeze of their passing ruffled his black hair, his long-fingered hands on the wheel.

She didn't care where they were going—she was with

Dominic, and that was enough— She asked, 'Where are we going?'

'There are many excellent restaurants in Venice, but as it's a nice evening I thought you might like to eat al fresco in Piazza San Marco.'

Remembering what he had said about that famous square, she said huskily, her cup running over, 'I'd love to.'

They disembarked at San Marco, but instead of holding her hand Dominic tucked it under his arm as they walked through the winding lanes.

'Palazzo Ducale, you'll certainly recognise,' he said as they passed the wonderfully ornate façade of the Doge's Palace. 'And the Basilica di San Marco and the Campanile you can't miss, but if you're not planning to leave Venice in a month the sightseeing can wait until another time.'

His words, and the casual way they were spoken, made a little chill feather across her skin. But at this early stage in their relationship she could hardly expect him to declare that he would never let her leave. Just the fact that they were together again should be enough.

Together again... But how had he known where to find her? What had he been doing in the Ca' Malvasia? Unless he'd seen her going in and followed her?

Though if he had why hadn't he said so at once? And why had he assumed that they were neighbours without her telling him anything about John or inheriting the house...?

All at once the questions were back, thick as wasps around a jam pot. 'Dominic...' she began.

Reading her mind with frightening accuracy, he stopped and put a finger to her lips. 'Explanations can come later, after we've eaten.'

Her heart racing, and made breathless by that lightest of touches, she resolutely turned her back on the questions.

Why spoil the evening by worrying? She would put the whole thing out of her mind until he was ready to tell her.

Simply enjoy being here with him, in this wonderfully romantic setting. Enjoy the happiness that Sophia's ring seemed to be bringing.

Though the sun no longer beat down, the sky, laced with ribbons of gold diaphanous cloud, still held a shimmering heat which hung like an inverted copper bowl over the square.

The café Dominic had chosen seemed fairly crowded, but in a trice a table was found for them and set up.

As they took their seats and ordered a flock of pigeons rose with a whirring of wings and wheeled, dark silhouettes against the brightness.

Sitting sipping a martini, looking at the wonderful façade of St Mark's and listening to the orchestra playing Neapolitan love songs, she burst out impulsively, 'I've never been so happy.'

For an instant he looked startled, almost disconcerted. Then a shutter came down and, his face wiped clear of all expression, he said lightly, 'Just wait until you taste the *soglione alla Veneziana.*'

When the waiter had cleared away the aperitif glasses and brought a carafe of chilled white wine, Dominic asked politely, 'Will you excuse me for a couple of minutes? I need to make a phone call, and I've forgotten to bring my mobile.'

'Of course.'

She watched as, tall and broad-shouldered, he threaded his way lithely between the tables and disappeared inside.

Day was dying now, swathed in the first blue-purple veils of approaching dusk, and the lights were coming on in the square. Music, talk and laughter swirled and eddied, while perfume and the aroma of roasting coffee mingled with a warm salt breeze from the Lagoon.

'*Buona sera, signorina.*' A strange young man was standing smiling down at her. 'Remember me?'

Belatedly, she recognised the white teeth and soulful brown eyes. *Mario.*

'Of course I remember you.' She returned his smile.

'You permit?'

Before she could point out that she was with someone, he had dropped into the chair opposite, his melting gaze never leaving her face.

'Did you find your hotel without difficulty?'

'Yes, *grazie.*'

'I should have come with you and carried your case. It was shameful of me to leave so beautiful a girl to make her own way.'

Made uncomfortable by his attitude, she said briskly, 'It really wasn't a problem.'

'And now you are here all on your own, on your very first evening—'

'But I'm not—'

In full flow, he carried on as though she hadn't spoken, 'I called at the hotel to find you, but they said you were not there. Then, as though it was meant to be, I find you sitting alone in Piazza San Marco.'

Seizing her hand, he added, 'It will be dark in a little while. You must allow me to take you on a gondola, show you what a very romantic place Venezia can be—'

Trying, without success, to free her hand, she interrupted, 'Mario, please listen to me...' Her words tailed off as she saw Dominic standing a few feet away watching silently.

The look of cold fury on his face made her flinch.

Seeing the movement, and following her gaze, Mario rose hastily to his feet, his eyes reproaching her.

'I'm sorry,' she said. 'I tried to tell you I wasn't alone.'

Dominic took a step forward and, with a muttered, '*Scusi,*' Mario lost no time in escaping.

'Dear me,' Dominic said, resuming his seat, 'I seem to have frightened your latest conquest away.'

Though he spoke lightly, and his face was now inscrutable, she could tell that he was still furiously angry. But surely there was no need for such an extreme reaction?

Wishing the little incident had never taken place, she said carefully, 'There's really no need to talk about conquests. He's just a young man who carried my case to the *vaporetto* earlier today.'

'He seemed to…shall we say…fancy his chances.'

'Well, I did nothing to encourage him, if that's what you're suggesting. He's a mere boy,' she added.

'Don't tell me you think age matters?' Dominic's voice had an edge to it. Before she could answer, he went on, 'And if all this young man did was carry your case to the landing stage, how did he know where you were staying?'

Aware of a little thrill of excitement, because he was acting like a jealous boyfriend, she told him, 'Carlo asked, so he could give me directions…'

Dominic raised a dark brow. 'Another one?'

'Carlo, who is Mario's brother, must be all of eleven or twelve. When I stopped in Piazzale Roma he offered to guard my case while I parked the car…'

By the time she finished describing the incident, Dominic had relaxed and was looking amused.

A few seconds later their food arrived and, back on an even keel, Nicola was able to enjoyed the meal, the wine and the sheer delight of being with him.

By the time they reached the coffee stage, the evening had turned oppressively hot and sultry.

Glancing up at the sky, which had darkened and grown heavy with massing columns of indigo cloud, Dominic remarked evenly, 'There's going to be a storm before too long, so I think it's time for a few questions and answers… If you'd like to begin?'

She started with the most puzzling. 'I don't understand how you found me… I can only presume you must have seen me in Campo dei Cavalli and followed me into the Ca' Malvasia?'

'Wrong on both counts.'

'You *didn't* follow me?'

'No.'

'Then you must have noticed that the door had been left open and, knowing the house was empty, decided to come in and investigate?'

Already he was shaking his head, his white smile making it into some kind of game.

'But I heard it slam as I reached the top of the stairs.'

'I didn't come that way.'

'So how *did* you get in?'

'At one time Ca' Malvasia used to be part of the Palazzo dei Cavalli...'

Of course. The old lady she had spoken to in the *campo* had said as much.

'When they were divided, a communicating door was left. I came through that way.'

Unable to credit it, she protested, 'You're not trying to tell me that our meeting like that was a coincidence? You *must* have known I was there—'

His eyes gleamed. 'Yes, I did. Or at least I knew you were going to be.'

Aware that he was playing with her, she said shortly, 'So it was your intention to lie in wait for me and scare me half to death?'

'No, that wasn't my intention. I would have come downstairs to meet you, but I was held up. As it was, I'd just come through the door at the end of the corridor, and when I realised you were so close I was almost as surprised as you were. Not *that* many women would have gone exploring a strange house in the dark.'

'How did you know I was coming to Ca' Malvasia? I

hadn't mentioned it.' Another thought struck her. 'And how did you know exactly *when* I'd be there?'

'I've been having you kept under surveillance.'

'What?' she said stupidly.

Calmly he repeated the statement.

'You've been having me watched…?' Choking with indignation, she demanded, 'Since when?'

'For the last couple of weeks,' he admitted with no sign of remorse.

'But we've only known each other two days,' she said blankly.

'We only *met* yesterday, but I've known about you for some time.'

'What do you mean, *known about me*? And *why* have you been having me watched?'

'As we're going to be neighbours—that is, unless you decide to sell—I wanted to know exactly what you were up to, what kind of person you were.'

'How did you know we were going to be neighbours? I've never mentioned having a house in Venice.'

'I thought you were about to… The evening we were at the Schloss Lienz.'

Recalling Innsbruck, and all that had happened there, she said with difficulty, 'So it wasn't just by chance that you were staying at the Bregenzerwald and in the next room?'

'No, it was all pre-planned.'

Feeling her blood turn to ice in her veins, she asked, 'How did you manage it?'

'Signor Mancini arranged everything…'

Just the fact that Signor Mancini was involved explained how Dominic had known she was going to be his neighbour… And remembering how politely insistent the solicitor had been about selecting her hotels and making all her reservations, Nicola bit her lip. Sandy hadn't been far wrong when she'd referred to the man as a slimy git.

With a slight smile, Dominic added, 'Apart from our actual introduction, that is.'

'What if I hadn't caught my heel and fallen on you?'

'I would have found some other way to get to know you. But as fate took a hand...'

CHAPTER FIVE

COLD through and through, despite the heat, she said, 'As you were on the spot so opportunely, you must have been following me.'

'I was,' he admitted coolly. 'At that point, wanting to make personal contact, I gave Muller another job to do.'

Muller... As he spoke the name, in her mind's eye she saw the bullet-headed man who had been sitting in the foyer at the Bregenzerwald.

Then a different man, short and blue-jowled, who had stared at her in the Piazzale Roma, and who, she was now sure, had been watching the hotel and had followed her to Ca' Malvasia. A man who had carried a mobile phone—that was how Dominic had known what time she would be there—and in all probability had been responsible for the door slamming.

She shivered. The fact that Dominic had had someone watching her every move, and reporting back, was becoming frighteningly clear.

What wasn't at all clear was *why...*

Keeping her voice as steady as possible, she said, 'You seem to have gone to a great deal of trouble and expense to have me checked out...'

'And you'd like to know why?'

'Yes.'

'I thought you might have guessed.'

'It's obviously something to do with the house. Though I don't see why my possibly becoming your neighbour should count as—'

'There's a little more to it than that.' His chiselled mouth twisted in a mirthless smile. 'The thing that does count is the fact that you might possibly have become, in a round-about way, my stepmother.'

'Your stepmother?'

'I presume you would have married John, had he lived?'

'Married John…? No, certainly not. The idea is quite absurd!'

Her reaction was so instinctive that just for an instant Dominic looked jolted.

'So you had no intention of actually marrying him?'

'Of course I hadn't… But just supposing I had, how could that possibly have made me your—?' She stopped speaking abruptly.

He waited, his grey eyes on her face.

'Sophia was your mother.'

'That's right.'

'But John wasn't your father.'

'Right again. My mother was married twice.'

'Yes, I know, John said so. But he'd never once mentioned having any stepchildren.'

'I rather thought not. You didn't even blink when I told you my name. And of course *children* is hardly the word. David was thirteen and I was twenty-one when they met and married. I'd just returned from college, and it was rather sprung on me…'

She got the distinct impression that had he been at home at the time he would have done his best to prevent it.

'I was aware that my mother had met someone, but they hadn't known each other for more than a few weeks, and I'd failed to realise it was serious.'

Something about the set of his mouth made her hazard, 'You didn't like John very much?'

He avoided the question, answering obliquely, 'It didn't much matter whether I liked him or not. My mother didn't ask for my approval.'

Greatly daring, Nicola queried, 'If she had, would you have given it?'

'No.' Dominic's answer was uncompromising. 'It had all happened too quickly. I thought he was probably marrying her for her money... You see, all the money was hers. As an only child she had inherited the Loredan fortune. My father, Richard Irving, had worked hard and added to it, and when he died, my mother was one of the richest women in Venice.'

Troubled, Nicola said with certainty, 'John absolutely adored her. I don't believe for a minute that he married her for her money.'

'It's possible I was wrong... But for a while things were awkward, and when I returned from my travels there was some friction. That's why the *palazzo* was divided and Ca' Malvasia came into existence.'

'I'm sure they were very happy there.'

As though striving to be fair, Dominic admitted, 'They appeared to be, and he seemed devastated when she died.' Cynically, he added, 'Though that might have been because, instead of being able to control the whole of her fortune, he was only left a third of it. The other two thirds stayed in the family. The palazzo and one third came to me, the rest was put in trust for David for when he reaches the age of thirty.'

'But you couldn't have been thirty when your mother died,' she objected.

Flatly, he said, 'I was twenty-six, and wealthy in my own right. David was eighteen, and still a bit wild. Mother's intention was to preserve the family fortune...'

Suddenly realising exactly where this was leading, Nicola sat quite still.

'Which was why John Turner's estate was supposed to come *back* to the family when he died.'

'I see,' Nicola said slowly, while her heart seemed to shrivel inside her.

With just those few words Dominic had made his interests clear, and crushed any hopes she might have cherished for the future.

She wanted to put her head down on her arms and cry her heart out.

It seemed that even the house and the money John had willed to her weren't rightfully hers...

But in that case why had both the solicitors, even Signor Mancini, who was obviously working for Dominic, let it go through?

But perhaps Dominic's claim was on moral rather than legal grounds? If it *was*, that put things in a somewhat different perspective.

While she wouldn't like to be morally responsible for leaving someone poor who ought to have been rich, as it stood she wasn't seriously depriving either Dominic or his brother.

Both already had a third their mother had willed to them and, in addition to that, Dominic had admitted to being a wealthy man in his own right. If he simply wanted John's share to increase what was already a substantial fortune...

Though Nicola was quiet and vulnerable in a lot of ways, she was far from weak. From her grandmother she had inherited an inner strength, a fine core of steel that, when the chips were down, made her a fighter.

She sat up straighter, unconsciously squaring her shoulders. 'You say John's estate was supposed to come back to the family?'

'Yes.'

'And you blame *me* because it didn't?'

'Not altogether.' Sardonically, he added, 'A young widow has to think about her future.'

It wasn't the answer she was hoping for, and, disliking

the connotations, she harked back to ask, 'What exactly do you mean by supposed?'

'It was understood that it should.'

'All of it? But surely John must have had money in his own right? He once told me that the London house, which he'd recently sold, was the family home and had belonged to his parents.'

Looking less than pleased, Dominic said, 'Well, if not all of it, certainly the money Mother left him, plus Ca' Malvasia. That was the understanding.'

'Whose understanding? Yours? Or everyone else involved?'

'Everyone else involved, as far as I know.'

'As far as you know? Didn't you talk to John about it?'

'No, I didn't,' Dominic replied a shade curtly.

'Or your mother?'

'My mother was a woman who liked to run her own affairs.'

'And she would have considered it interfering?'

Watching his jaw tighten, Nicola knew she'd struck a nerve.

Ignoring the question, he said repressively, 'It was her wish that the Loredan estate should remain intact. Which meant that John's share, and particularly Ca' Malvasia, should be returned to the family.'

'Was that stipulated in her will?'

'It should have been.'

Those four words answered Nicola's question.

On firmer ground now, she fought back, 'If your mother had seriously intended her husband's share to be returned to the family, surely it would have been?'

His grey eyes cold as ice, Dominic said, 'I can only presume that she relied upon him to respect her wishes. And at that time it probably didn't seem necessary. He had no other family. No children of his own. No one to leave it to.

Who could have guessed that he would lose his head over a girl young enough to be his daughter?'

'You've got it all wrong,' Nicola informed him coldly. 'John didn't *lose his head* over me. There was absolutely nothing of that kind about our relationship.'

'You didn't love him?'

'John was special, and I cared about him. But I didn't *love* him, at least not in the way you mean. We were just good friends.'

Seeing a sardonic half smile twist Dominic's firm lips, she assured him, 'And that's the truth, believe me...' Then was angry with herself for sounding defensive.

'How long had you known each other?'

Convinced that he already knew the answer, she admitted, 'About six months.'

'Did you live together?' The sudden question was like a whiplash.

Green eyes flashed. 'No, we didn't! The whole idea is absurd! John was more than twice my age.'

'What does age have to do with it? Some women are able to attract men of any age from sixteen to sixty... As you've already amply demonstrated.'

The rider made her flinch. So that was the kind of woman he believed her to be, she thought despairingly. And the unfortunate episode with Mario had only served to strengthen that belief.

Dominic's reaction, rather than being the jealous anger she had read it as, had simply been a wholesome disgust.

Biting her lip, she said with difficulty, 'I can understand in a way why you think that. But you're quite wrong. I'm not like that at all. And as far as John goes, as I've just said, it wasn't that kind of relationship. We were each of us travelling, and during the months we knew each other we only met up three or four times. Occasionally he'd phone or write, and once we had dinner together when we both happened to be in London at the same time…'

'Do you honestly expect me to believe that's all there was to it? That it was quite innocent?'

'Whether you believe it or not, it happens to be the truth.'

'Why should a man who was far from being a fool leave everything he possessed to a girl he'd only met half a dozen times at the most? Of course, if he was besotted, and the girl had…shall we say *encouraged* him by promising to marry him…'

It was oppressively hot and sticky. Pushing back a wisp of hair that had escaped and clung damply to her cheek, Nicola denied firmly, 'He wasn't besotted, and I've already told you there was never any question of marriage.'

'So what did you promise?'

Almost wearily, she said, 'I didn't promise anything. John loved his wife very dearly and—'

'That might well be true. But she'd been dead for almost four years—'

'She might have been dead for four years, but he still hadn't got over her death.'

'He wasn't an old man. Only in his late fifties. He might well have considered taking a lover. Felt he needed a woman in his life—'

Nicola shook her head. 'You must know that John was already suffering from a bad heart.' Though aware that Dominic looked surprised, as if he *hadn't* known, she pressed on, 'The only thing he needed at that point was a friend. Someone in the same boat who could appreciate his loss and understand what he was going through…'

There was a far-off growl of thunder and sheet lightning flickered in the distance. The very air seemed to be holding its breath, waiting for the coming storm.

Her head had begun to ache savagely, and, feeling unable to cope any longer, she pushed back her chair and gathered up her bag. 'If you'll excuse me... I'm getting rather tired and I'd like to go.'

He rose immediately, once more the polished host. 'Then of course I'll take you home.'

'Thank you,' she said with stilted politeness. 'But there's really no need. I can get a water-taxi.'

'Not at all.' He was equally polite. 'I won't hear of it.'

Signalling a waiter, he paid the bill before offering her his arm.

Her ankle had stiffened up and was hurting, but, pretending not to notice the proffered arm, she set off towards the *piazzetta*, hurrying in her need to get away, disregarding the pain.

With Dominic keeping pace effortlessly, they walked a foot apart, like strangers, to where the boat was moored.

He jumped in first and turned. His whole attitude was challenging, and she was tempted to ignore the hand he held out to her.

But the amount of traffic on the lagoon was making the dark water choppy, and the small craft was bobbing about like a cork on a rough sea.

A flash of lightning silhouetted Dominic, standing with his legs a little apart, balancing with the grace of familiarity. Making it look easy.

Still she doubted her ability to step in unaided. It wasn't something she was *used* to doing, and if her ankle let her down and she had to be ignominiously fished out of the lagoon, he would certainly have the last laugh...

Admitting defeat, she took his hand.

As she stepped in, either the boat lurched or he gave a little pull, and, completely off balance, she fell against him.

He took her weight easily, and for a moment or two held her pressed against the length of his muscular body.

Finding her footing, she pulled herself free and, glad that

it was dark enough to hide her flaming face, sat down with a bump.

His soft laugh convincing her it had been no accident, but his way of paying her back, she sat in stony silence as they began their journey.

She hadn't mentioned where she was staying, but obviously he knew. Either Signor Mancini or the man who had been following her would no doubt have told him, she thought bitterly.

The low rumbles of thunder and the distant flashes of lightning indicated that the storm was still some way away; Dominic was taking the quieter canals and driving without haste.

Where two waterways intersected, they were held up by a red traffic light. As they waited for it to change to green, some warning sixth sense made Nicola query, 'We are going the right way?'

She saw his white teeth gleam in a mocking smile. 'I was taking the quieter route, on the grounds that at night it's more romantic.'

Wishing she hadn't asked, she relapsed into silence.

The back canals, with only a few lamps gleaming on the dark water, tended to look very much alike, and she soon lost all track of where they were.

Watching for the distinctive humpbacked bridge she had crossed earlier that evening, and the main entrance to the Hotel Lunga, she was taken by surprise when Dominic suddenly cut the engine and turned into a well-lit boat-house.

As he drew into the landing stage and reached to moor the craft, she cried, 'What are you doing? This isn't the hotel.'

'I never thought it was,' he assured her gravely.

Making an effort to keep the panic from her voice, she protested, 'But you were supposed to be taking me home.'

'This *is* home,' he said, as he handed her out and helped her onto the landing stage.

Jerking her hand free, she said bitterly, 'It might be *your* home, but it's not mine. I didn't want to come back here.'

Ignoring her protest, he turned and led the way up the steps and into the *palazzo*, leaving her little choice but to follow him.

When they reached the hall, he asked politely, 'Would you like to come through to my study for a nightcap of some kind?'

'No, I wouldn't,' she answered raggedly. 'I want to go back to the hotel. If you won't take me I'll get a water-taxi.'

'Well, you could—'

'I certainly will.'

'But I wouldn't advise it,' he carried on smoothly. 'As it's the height of the tourist season, you're hardly likely to get a room.'

'I've *got* a room.'

'Not any more. I told them they could let someone else have it.'

'You *what*?'

'I explained that as you'd had a slight accident while visiting Ca' Malvasia, I'd invited you to stay at Palazzo dei Cavalli.'

'I don't *want* to stay here!' she cried, overcome with agitation at the thought. 'Besides, all my belongings are still at the hotel.'

He shook his head. 'I asked for them to be brought over. You'll find that everything is in your room, waiting for you.'

'No, I refuse to stay! I'm going to get my things and leave.'

'It's almost twelve o'clock,' he pointed out levelly. 'You can't go walking around Venice alone at this time of night with a sprained ankle. And don't pretend there's nothing wrong with it, because I know quite well there is.'

'*Please*, Dominic...'

Quizzically, he asked, 'Is the prospect of being my guest distressing enough to make you beg?'

'I don't care to be the guest of a man who's convinced I'm nothing but a heartless, scheming gold-digger.' Her voice broke. 'I don't even know why you *want* me here.'

But even as she spoke she knew only too well why. It would enable him to keep her under surveillance more easily...

'Let's just say you fascinate me.'

He sounded sincere and, thrown, she momentarily dropped her defences.

Taking immediate advantage, he cupped her elbow and, urging her into his study, helped her off with her loose jacket before pushing her gently onto the couch.

Lit only by several standard lamps, the large, well-furnished room had an air of cosy intimacy that had been lacking earlier.

Crouching at her feet, Dominic slipped off her sandals. 'Now, let me take a look at that ankle.'

It had puffed up considerably, and become so stiff and painful that she was forced to bite her lip as his long fingers began to gently probe and press.

Clicking his tongue in annoyance, he said, 'I should have had the sense to make you stay indoors and rest it...'

In spite of everything it gave her the strangest feeling—a combination of excitement, desire and tenderness—to look down at his bent head. The thick black hair that gleamed with health and wanted to curl, the tiny ends that feathered into his tanned nape... Even the back of his neck was sexy...

Glancing up, he added, 'I think a cold compress is called for.'

His eyes lingered on her face, and as though what she had been thinking was written there for him to read she felt herself start to blush.

Finding it an unexpectedly sweet amusement to tease her, Dominic watched with interest while she turned red as a poppy.

Then, rising to his feet with effortless grace, he said, 'I'll only be a minute,' and disappeared through the door, leaving it open behind him.

Disturbed and angry with herself, she wished fervently that she could just get up and walk out.

But even if Dominic would allow her to, she couldn't go wandering round a strange city with nowhere to go and a storm brewing.

Though she hated the feeling of being a prisoner, she would be much safer here.

Or would she? It would all depend on what kind of safety she was thinking of…

He was back quite quickly, with a cold pad and a crêpe bandage which he applied with deft efficiency. Nicola was surprised by his competence. In her admittedly small experience of men, most of them could hardly cope with a sticking plaster.

Watching his lean, well-shaped hands tuck in the end of the bandage and fasten it neatly with a safety pin, she went hot, her skin burning as she recalled what pleasure those skilful hands could bring…

'There, that should improve matters.'

His voice made her jump.

'Thank you.' Aware that in her agitation she had sounded ungracious, she added jerkily, 'I'm sure it will.'

'Now, what about that nightcap?'

Eager to escape, she shook her head. 'I don't think so. Really… I'm ready for bed.'

'There's not much point in going to bed wound tight as

a spring. You're much more likely to sleep if you put your feet up and relax for half an hour while you have a drink.'

Though phrased as a suggestion, she felt sure it was an order and, convinced that if she didn't put her feet up he would have no qualms about doing it for her, she reluctantly obeyed.

'So what's it to be? A brandy?'

She shook her head. 'Something long, cold and non-alcoholic, please.'

He went to a sideboard that contained a small fridge, and after a moment returned with a glass of iced fruit juice.

'How's that?'

She took a sip and said, 'Lovely.' Then, on edge because he was watching her, sat rolling the beaded coldness of the glass between her hot palms.

Frowning a little, he remarked, 'You look as if your headache's come back?'

'Yes, it has,' she admitted.

He took a small bottle from his pocket, and after unscrewing the cap shook a couple of tablets into her palm. 'You'd better have another couple of these.'

'Thank you.' Obediently she put them in her mouth and, taking another sip of her drink, swallowed. They failed to go down and she shuddered as they dissolved bitterly on her tongue.

Well aware that he was still standing studying her intently, and needing something to say, she asked, 'Your housekeeper doesn't object to having an unexpected *guest* thrust on her?'

'Not at all,' Dominic answered evenly. 'For some reason she approves of you.'

'How do you know?'

'Because she chose to get your room ready herself. By the time I rang to make sure your belongings had arrived, she assured me that everything was in order.'

Discarding his jacket, he undid his black tie, leaving the ends dangling, and unfastened the top two buttons of his white silk evening shirt, exposing the tanned column of his throat.

Nicola shivered, recalling all too clearly how she had buried her mouth against it while his hands had roamed at will over her eager body...

Catching sight of her rapt face, and intrigued by it, Dominic watched as her pupils grew large and unfocused, her soft lips parted and a slight flush stained her high cheekbones.

Innocently erotic, she looked like a woman being made love to.

It had a powerful effect on him and, forced to leash his own sexuality, he wondered who the man was who had engendered that look. Possibly her husband. Though he doubted it.

Suddenly she blinked, and, coming back to the present to find his eyes were fixed on her face, hastily looked down.

Her small, straight nose was shiny and there was a faint dew of perspiration on her forehead and upper lip, while the lamp she was sitting under shone on her corn-coloured hair and cast shadows of her long lashes onto her cheeks.

She really was quite enchanting, he thought. No wonder John had been captivated by her. If only she was half as innocent as she looked...

But everything seemed to suggest that, far from being innocent, she was a clever manipulator who used her beauty to further her own ends.

Unconsciously, he sighed.

There was a gleaming coffee-making machine on the sideboard, and reaching for a small cup he made himself some espresso before taking a seat opposite his unwilling guest.

For a while they sipped in silence, then, picking up the

threads of their earlier conversation, he said, 'So John had developed a bad heart? Could nothing be done about it?'

'No, it was just a matter of time. You didn't know?'

He shook his head. 'But I find it interesting that *you* did…'

So he thought she had battened on to a middle-aged man whom she had *expected* to die.

After a moment, Dominic went on flatly, 'As soon as Mother's funeral was over he closed up the house and left. Apart from one brief exchange, we hadn't been in touch since.'

No wonder John had never mentioned having a family. Clearly there had been no love lost on either side, and after his wife's death there would have been nothing to keep him in Venice…

'Where and when did you two meet?'

Dominic's question broke into her thoughts, and, collecting herself, she answered, 'In Paris, at the end of last November.'

'Tell me about it.' Whimsically, he added, 'And I'm a glutton for detail.'

Well, if it was detail he wanted, he should have it.

'Linda Atkin, one of my fellow workers at Westlake, who was organising a heads of business conference in Paris, had been taken seriously ill with pneumonia… I forget which hospital the ambulance took her to. Possibly it was Saint Antoine's…'

Dominic's small twisted smile acknowledged her mockery.

'Anyway, at very short notice I was asked to fly to Paris and take over her duties. The conference was being held at the Hotel Honfleur, which is one of the older-type, greystone hotels in the Rue Rosslare, not far from the Champs Elysées…'

Holding up both hands in a gesture of surrender, he said, 'Okay, I'm sorry. I should have said *relevant* detail.'

Unwilling to let him have it all his own way, she asked, 'Suppose we have different ideas on what we regard as relevant?'

'I'll go along with what *you* consider is.'

With saccharine sweetness, she said, 'You're too kind.'

Judging by the gleam in his eye, he would have liked to take her over his knee, but he only said politely, 'Do go on.'

'There were some fifty delegates at the conference, which was due to start the following morning, and most of them had already arrived and been settled in. But as far as I was concerned, with not coming on the scene until quite late that evening, there was still a lot to check over. On the ground floor, next door to the conference facilities, there was a small office to work in, which was a great help. Unfortunately, some last-minute problems meant it was very late by the time I'd got everything sorted out.

'Tired, and none too warm, I was about to go up to my room, which was on the fourth floor, when I discovered there had been some kind of power failure and the lifts weren't working. Which meant I had no choice but to walk up…'

The whole place was silent and deserted at that time in the morning, and Nicola had almost reached the fourth floor landing when the sight of a man slumped on the stairs made her jump.

A middle-aged man, dressed conventionally in a grey business suit and tie, was sitting on the third step from the top, leaning against the wall, head bent.

Her first thought was that if he had had too much to drink she would need to call someone. But there had been no sign of any night staff.

As she hesitated, he muttered, 'Sophia,' and lifted his head.

He was a nice-looking man, somewhere in his late fifties, she guessed, with a lean, ascetic face, thick grizzled hair and hazel eyes.

It was immediately clear that he was ill rather than drunk. His face was ashen, the skin stretched tightly over the bones, and his lips were blue.

'How can I help?' she asked in English.

She was about to repeat the question in French when he answered, 'Tablets.'

'Which pocket?'

He made a fumbling gesture. 'Top, inside…' His face was contorted with pain and the breath rasped in his throat.

Sitting on the cold marble step beside him, she felt in his top right-hand jacket pocket and gave a sigh of relief when her fingers closed around a small plastic container.

'Two?'

'Yes.'

She shook two of the tiny white tablets into her palm and watched him clumsily pick them up and put them under his tongue.

Wishing she was carrying her mobile phone, she said quickly, 'I'll go and call an ambulance.'

As she half rose he grasped her hand with a kind of desperate strength, pulling her down again. 'Stay with me, please.'

The fingers gripping hers were like ice.

Wondering how long he'd been there, she said, 'You really ought to have some help.'

'N-nothing they can do,' he mumbled.

Afraid that if she left him he might somehow tumble down the stairs, she stayed where she was.

Holding his hand between both of hers, she tried to warm

it, while she went over in her mind how to do heart massage should it become necessary.

But the tablets appeared to be working, and after a little while that dreadful ashen look began to disappear and his colour gradually seeped back.

Despite the returning colour, she saw that his face looked pinched and cold.

It was freezing in the stairwell, which suggested that the central heating had stopped working at the same time as the lifts.

She herself was starting to feel chilled to the bone and, concerned for him, knowing it would be better if they could move, she asked, 'How are you feeling?'

'Better now. Just need to lie down.'

'Which floor are you on?'

'The seventh.'

Only too aware that there was no way he could climb three flights of stairs in that condition, she said, 'You'd better lie down in my room for a while…'

Once he was safely lying down, she could go in search of some assistance.

'It's quite close,' she added reassuringly. 'Just through this door and we're practically there.'

A quick look in her shoulder bag located her room key and she slipped it into the pocket of her suit before offering him her arm.

With her help he got unsteadily to his feet.

'You can lean on me,' she said. 'I'm much stronger than I look.'

Though he was quite tall, he was spare, and, his arm around her shoulders, they somehow made it through the door and the few steps down the carpeted corridor to her room.

Once inside, she steered him to the bed and drew back the duvet. He sank down on the side, and she slipped off his shoes and socks before helping him remove his jacket and tie and undoing the top two buttons of his shirt.

'Do you need anything else?'

'Nothing else.'

When he was lying down, she made him as comfortable as possible and pulled the duvet over him, before switching off the main light and adjusting the bedside lamp so that it didn't shine in his face.

'There, now you can get some rest.'

His eyes closed, he said huskily, 'Thank you, my dear. You've been very kind.'

She was about to move away when he reached blindly for her hand. Suddenly, urgently, he said, 'Stay with me. I don't want to be alone.'

'I should get some help... A doctor...'

'No use...' His fingers tightened painfully. 'Promise you won't leave me.'

Touched by his need, she said, 'I promise.'

Still holding his hand, she sank down in the small arm-chair by the bed and, leaning back against the cushion, waited for him to sleep...

CHAPTER SIX

WHEN Nicola opened her eyes and peered blearily at her watch, she found it was a quarter past six.

The man in her bed was still asleep. His breathing was easy, and she was relieved to see that his colour was good.

She felt stiff and cramped through sleeping in an awkward position. There was a crick in her neck, and her right arm had pins and needles.

One good thing was that some time during the night the heating had come back on and the room was comfortably warm.

Moving carefully, she collected a change of clothing and went into the bathroom, quietly closing the door behind her.

When she was showered and dressed, her hair taken up in its usual smooth coil, she returned to the bedroom to find her unexpected guest had awakened and was sitting on the edge of the bed putting on his shoes.

He looked up to smile at her. 'Good morning.'

'Good morning.' She returned his smile. 'How are you feeling this morning?'

'Right as rain, thank you.'

'I'm so pleased,' she told him, and meant it.

'I must apologise for all the trouble I've caused you.'

She shook her head. 'It was no trouble.'

'You gave me your bed... Where did you sleep?'

'In the chair.'

Seeing he looked worried, she reassured him, 'And quite soundly, I might add. I've only just showered and dressed.'

'Something I'm about to do.'

Recalling that he was on the seventh floor, she said, 'I'd better just check to see if the lifts are working again.'

To her relief they were, and she returned to report, 'Whatever the problem was, they seem to have fixed it.'

'Good. I'm afraid I'm not really up to stairs.'

Taking his jacket from the back of the chair, he shrugged it on, then coiled his tie and slipped it into his pocket.

Holding out his hand, he said, 'You've been very good to me, and I don't even know your name.'

'Nicola Whitney.'

'I'm John Turner.'

They shook hands gravely.

'Are you here for the conference?' she asked.

'Yes. Are you?'

'I'm organising it. A last-minute replacement for Miss Atkin, who was taken ill yesterday afternoon.'

'I suppose that means you have to start work very early?'

'Not too early. I got most of the details sorted out last night.'

'In that case, will you have breakfast with me?' A shade gruffly, he added, 'There still seems to be a lot to say.'

Since Jeff's death she had assiduously avoided social contacts, so she was surprised to hear herself agreeing, 'Thank you, I'd like to.'

'Then shall we say the breakfast room in fifteen minutes' time?'

After checking through the day's agenda, Nicola went down to the breakfast room, which was at the rear and looked over an enclosed garden.

It was still quite early, and the only other occupant was a man dunking a roll into a cup of hot chocolate while he read the morning paper.

The glass roof and the amount of windows suggested that the room had originally been built as a conservatory. This notion was reinforced by a pale tiled floor and a profusion of tall green plants and potted palms.

Skirting round a particularly luxuriant fern, Nicola chose a table for two over by the windows.

When, a moment or two later, John Turner walked in, freshly shaved and wearing a well-cut suit, it was like seeing an old friend.

He sat down opposite and smiled at her. His mouth and teeth were good, and she thought afresh what a nice-looking man he was.

A waiter appeared to take their order of orange juice, coffee and croissants, and returned almost immediately with a loaded tray.

While they spread *confiture* on the fresh, flaky croissants, they talked easily about the conference and the day ahead.

Nicola had poured their second cup of coffee before John introduced a personal note, by saying abruptly, 'With regard to last night... I must apologise.'

'Apologise? For what?'

'I have the distinct impression that I clung to you like a child.'

'There's absolutely nothing to apologise for,' she assured him.

'Thank you. You're very kind.'

'Isn't there anything...?' she paused uncertainly.

Reading her mind, he shook his head. 'Because of several different factors my condition is terminal, and every attack takes me a step closer. I know and accept that. But, while I was prepared to die, I suddenly found I didn't want to die alone. Perhaps it was the thought of going into the unknown...

'I've never been a religious man, and I can only hope that my wife was right when, on her deathbed, she promised she would be waiting for me.'

'Sophia?' Nicola said.

Looking startled, John asked, 'How did you know?'

'Last night when you were sitting on the stairs, you spoke her name.'

'I wanted her there with me... But instead you came, and I can never thank you enough.'

Then, with a determined change of subject, 'You must travel a lot in your job?'

'Yes, almost non-stop.'

'Don't you ever get tired of it?'

'Sometimes,' she admitted.

'I see you're married. Doesn't your husband mind you being away from home so much?'

Quietly, she said, 'My husband's dead. He was killed in a car crash.'

'How long ago?'

'Two and a half years.'

Reaching across the table, John took her hand. 'It doesn't get any easier, does it? It's three and a half years since my wife died, and I still miss her every hour of every day, as you must miss your husband...'

'So you and John forged an instant bond of sympathy?'

Dominic's quiet voice brought Nicola back to the present, and she blinked a little as the Honfleur's breakfast room, with its pale tiled floor and walls of glass, was replaced by the lamplit study.

'I'm sorry?'

He repeated the question.

'Yes, you could say that.'

'And I presume you went on to find out a great deal about each other?'

'Not exactly. John told me comparatively little about his private life. As I said earlier, he never once mentioned having a stepfamily. Or living in Venice, for that matter.'

'I wonder why not?'

'I think he still found it too painful to talk about Sophia and the past. We were in the same boat, so I could understand how he felt...'

'Then you really *had* lost your husband?'

As Nicola stared at him blankly, thinking that she must have misheard the question, he added, 'Or was that just a clever trick to gain sympathy and form a fast and easy rapport?'

Even then she wasn't sure she'd understood.

'I don't know what you mean,' she said.

'I mean, are you *really* a widow? Or is it just part of the act, so to speak?'

Every vestige of colour left her face, and, white to the lips, she said, 'I wish I could say it *was* just part of an act, but unfortunately I am a widow.' Her voice hoarse and impeded, she added, 'I told you all about my husband...'

'But how much of what you told me was actually true?'

Lifting her chin, she looked him in the eye. 'All of it. Every single word.'

Then, bitterly, 'Though knowing in what light you must have regarded me, I suppose I couldn't expect you to believe anything I told you.'

'I have to admit that by the time we left the Schloss Lienz I'd started to wonder if I could be wrong about you. Everything you'd said *sounded* convincing.'

Ironically, he added, 'In spite of all I knew to the contrary, I was almost on the point of believing in that innocent young girl—'

Suddenly furious, she choked, 'What do you mean, "in spite of all I knew to the contrary"? You didn't *know* anything. Because John left me his money, you *presumed* I must be a gold-digger who'd got her hooks into him. You jumped to conclusions that were completely false.'

A flash of lightning through the shutters and a louder

rumble of thunder brought their own touch of drama to the scene. The distant storm was circling round, getting closer.

'I'm sure you'd like me to think that you're as innocent as you look, but I'm afraid I can't.'

Stung, she said with blistering scorn, 'You've let the desire to hang on to your mother's fortune warp your judgement. You wouldn't recognise innocence if you fell over it.'

'But I can recognise *lack* of it,' he said evenly.

'What?'

'I can recognise *lack* of it,' he repeated.

His voice caustic, he went on, 'Surely you don't expect me to believe that someone as naive and innocent as you had painted yourself to be could later on that same evening throw herself at me quite so blatantly?'

Recalling all too clearly how she had swayed towards him and put her hands flat-palmed against his chest, Nicola felt her face flame.

'Or do you want to deny that too?'

'I know it must have *looked* as if I was throwing myself at you, but it was quite accidental. I just lost my balance.'

'Really?' he drawled.

'Yes, really.' Stammering a little, she tried to explain. 'I—I'm not used to drinking and I'd had too much wine, and then a cognac. It made me unsteady on my feet...'

His cynical expression told her clearly that he didn't believe a word of it.

'So you're saying it wasn't a come-on?'

'That's exactly what I'm saying.'

He smiled grimly. 'I suppose next you'll be swearing you didn't want to go to bed with me, and trying to blame me for seducing you?'

Looking down, she said in a small voice, 'No.'

Watching the fan of long, gold-tipped lashes flicker against the pure curve of her cheek, he echoed, 'No?'

'I've no intention of trying to blame you for seducing me.'

'I'm pleased to hear it.'

Gathering her courage, and knowing that her only option was to speak the truth, she went on, 'And though I didn't intend to invite it, I did want to go to bed with you.'

He raised a dark, mocking brow. 'Tell me, Nicola, do you feel the urge to sleep with every new man you meet?'

Her face burning afresh, she said, 'No, I don't. The only man I've ever slept with is my husband.'

'You mean apart from me?' he asked, a gleam in his grey eyes.

Lifting her chin, she agreed, 'Apart from you.'

Then, needing to convince him that she wasn't the kind of woman he thought her, she insisted quietly, 'Since Jeff died I've never so much as *looked* at another man.'

'Do you know, I could almost believe that?' he said with more than a touch of sarcasm.

'You *can* believe it.'

'Didn't you tell me that your husband had been dead for several years?'

'Three.'

'And you've been celibate all that time?'

'Yes.'

'A young and beautiful widow in need of consolation... Surely there must have been plenty of men who were interested?'

'Except for John, I avoided telling anyone I *was* a widow.'

Dominic's smile was twisted.

Recalling their first meeting, she added hastily, 'I mean until I met you.'

Desperate to make him understand, she went on, 'Apart from doing my job, I shut myself away from all contact with people. Men simply didn't interest me. I just wanted to be left alone to pick up the pieces.'

'Are you telling me that, as a young and healthy woman with natural needs, you didn't *miss* human contact?'

'If you mean sex—when you're grieving for someone sex becomes unimportant. It was the *warmth* of human contact, the *caring* that I missed.'

Her words held an unmistakable ring of truth, and for a heartbeat he looked distinctly shaken.

Then, his face expressionless, he asked, 'So if you had gone for three years without taking a lover, why indulge in just a casual romp with a perfect stranger?'

Feeling as if a giant hand was squeezing her heart, she stayed silent.

But, apparently intent on having an answer, he persisted, 'Or perhaps you're going to tell me that you felt I was *special*, like John Turner?'

'No, I'm not.' How could she tell him that? After he'd called it 'just a casual romp'.

'So why?'

'Too much to drink, perhaps. A sudden impulse. Or maybe a feeling that my time of mourning was finally over and I could start to live again.'

'Then almost any man would have done?'

'No!' Then, regretting her vehemence, 'It would have had to be someone I was really attracted to.'

'Ah! But then didn't you say your husband and I were alike?'

'I thought so at first, but I was wrong,' she stated flatly. 'You're not like Jeff at all. Not even in looks.'

He thought that over, before asking, 'All the same you were attracted to me?'

'Yes.'

When she failed to elaborate, he remarked silkily, 'I

thought you might have regarded me as another possible meal-ticket?'

'I don't need a meal-ticket.'

'Perhaps not, now your future's taken care of.'

'I never did need a meal-ticket,' she told him spiritedly. 'I'm quite capable of earning a living and taking care of the future myself.'

'Some women might consider that finding a rich and lonely man in failing health is an easy way to do it.'

'Some women might, but I don't happen to be one of them.'

As if she hadn't spoken, he went on, 'It's surprising how even an apparently level-headed man can be taken in by a beautiful face. Though isn't there a saying, there's no fool like an old fool?'

'John was far from being a fool. He *was* lonely, but even so, if I *had* been hoping to "take him in" I'm sure he would have known.'

'When did he actually tell you he was going to leave you his money?'

'He didn't. We never discussed money. I had no idea he was a rich man. The first I knew about it was when the solicitors wrote to tell me of his death and asked me to call in to see them.'

Then, knowing she would never convince him, and sick of trying, she swung her feet to the floor. 'Now, if you'll excuse me, it's been a long day and I really would like to go to bed.'

Dominic gave her a glinting, sidelong smile. 'But not alone, I hope?'

Wondering why a man like him wanted to take a woman he so obviously despised to bed, she said curtly, 'Definitely alone.'

'Oh, well...' With a shrug he rose to his feet, observing

casually, 'To avoid straining that ankle any further, I'd better carry you.'

'No!' Suddenly panic-stricken, she insisted, 'I can walk up. I don't need to be carried.'

Being carried up, held against his muscular body, would only weaken her resolve not to indulge in the kind of casual sex he had in mind.

And she mustn't *allow* herself to weaken.

To sleep with him again would destroy her pride and her self-respect. It would make her into the kind of woman he imagined her to be.

Despite the cold compress her ankle was still swollen and, realising it would be difficult to walk in heels, she decided to go barefooted. Picking up her sandals, she struggled to her feet.

She had taken just a couple of steps when her ankle let her down, and with a gasp of pain she dropped the sandals and grabbed the back of the nearest chair.

Dominic gave an exclamation of annoyance. 'Now perhaps you'll stop acting like a stubborn little fool!'

Before she could argue any further he had stooped and lifted her high in his arms.

In response, her stomach folded in on itself, every nerve-ending in her body sang into life, and her heartbeat and breathing both quickened drastically.

She was trying hard to appear unmoved when he gave her a sardonic glance and suggested, 'It would be a big help if you were to put your arms around my neck.'

Biting her lip, she reluctantly did as he'd asked, clasping her hands together behind his dark head. He had lifted her so effortlessly that, unable to believe he *needed* any help, she felt sure he was merely baiting her.

As he carried her across the hall and up a beautiful marble staircase that contrived to make the one in Ca' Malvasia seem relatively ordinary, her certainty that he was superbly fit was upheld.

His breathing had quickened only slightly, and she was oddly convinced that it was due to the feel of her body against his, rather than her weight. It verified the fact that, no matter how badly he thought of her, he still wanted her.

Why?

Or was it simply a case of any woman would do? But instinctively she felt that *wasn't* so.

When they reached the top of the grand staircase he turned left and followed a wide corridor hung with chandeliers. It was crossed by several smaller corridors and lined on either side with magnificent mirrors and paintings, and dark, elaborately carved doors.

He stopped in front of a door part-way along and, still holding her, said evenly, 'This is your room.'

There seemed to be no way of differentiating between them, and she wondered how on earth he knew which was which.

As though reading her mind, he asked, 'Is there something wrong?'

'Not really...' Determinedly looking away from the face so close to hers, she explained, 'Only it struck me that if I have to leave it I might have a problem finding it again...'

'It shouldn't be necessary to leave it, at least until morning. The old place has had a certain amount of modernisation, and all the rooms in this wing have an *en suite* bathroom.'

'Oh.' Feeling a bit foolish, she added, 'It's just that all the doors look alike.'

'At first glance they may *look* alike, but when you have time to study the carved panels you'll see that they're all different. Most of them represent Roman gods or deities, of which there were a vast number...'

With no change of tone, he queried, 'Perhaps you'd like to turn the doorknob?'

Unclasping her hands, she reached to do his bidding. While she turned the heavy metal knob, the fingers of the other hand brushed the short hair curling into his nape. Though thick and springy, it had the texture of silk. She wanted to keep on touching it.

Shouldering open the door, he carried her into a large, well-furnished room, where the hanging lamps had been left burning, and set her carefully on her feet. As he removed his hand it brushed against the side of her breast.

Though it seemed to have been accidental, just that casual touch made her nipples grow firm, and she found herself praying that he wouldn't notice the evidence of her arousal.

Luckily, his mind seemed to be on other things. 'All you need to do to know which is your room,' he continued, 'is look out for Janus.' He pointed to the central door panel, where a strong, mask-like carving showed two identical faces looking in opposite directions. 'As you can see he has two faces...'

With a strange inflection in his voice, he went on, 'I chose this room especially for you.'

As her colour rose, he added smoothly, 'But not for the reason you imagine...'

Smiling a little, he touched her warm cheek with cool fingers, destroying what remained of her composure.

'Janus is usually depicted with two faces as he is the guardian of doors, and every door looks two ways. January was named after him because he's also the god of new beginnings...'

New beginnings...

As she gazed at him, wondering if his words held some deeper meaning, he said lightly, 'When I asked what your plans were, didn't you answer that this holiday was to be a new beginning?'

'Yes, I did.'

And it had been. Though what had promised to be the start of a wonderful voyage of discovery had foundered on the rocks of Dominic's prejudice before it had even begun.

Then, because the need to know had been gnawing at her, 'I'd like *you* to answer a question now.'

'Very well. What do you want to know?'

The words practically tumbling over each other, yet instinctively careful how she phrased it, she asked, 'As you think so badly of me, why did you take me to bed last night?'

For an instant he looked disconcerted, then he admitted ruefully, 'I couldn't help myself. I wanted you so much that it was impossible to simply walk away.'

'I should have thought it would have been quite easy to walk away from a woman you had nothing but contempt for.'

'Oh, I wouldn't say *nothing* but contempt... I found you both disturbing and bewitching, and I was jealous of John... But, while I despised myself for feeling that way, I found I wanted you more than I'd ever wanted any other woman...'

She felt an almost fierce satisfaction. At least the *desire* had been mutual.

'I still do.' Standing quite still, he looked intensely into her lovely face. 'What do you want?'

She knew only too well what she wanted, and the recognition made her go hot all over.

His smile knowing, confident, he put his hands on her shoulders and drew her against him, eliciting by that simple act a more immediate and urgent desire than Jeff had ever evoked in all the months they had been married.

Reading her reaction, he bent his dark head to kiss her, but even as her lips parted and she felt her body grow limp and pliant her mind was suddenly clear, icy cool.

Jerking herself free, she said, 'What *I* want is for you to believe that I'm not the kind of woman you think I am.'

Though obviously startled, he made a swift recovery. 'I'd *like* to believe you're as innocent as the day is long, but in the circumstances that seems highly improbable... However, I'm willing to give you the benefit of the doubt while we get to know each other better.'

Stung, she said quietly, 'You really are an arrogant swine.'

He laughed, and with his index finger lightly traced her cheek and jawline. 'But you still want to sleep with me?'

Tempted almost beyond endurance, she clenched her teeth. But knowing that if she appeared to be easy it would only serve to confirm his bad opinion of her, she denied firmly, 'No, I don't.'

'Sure? It's one of the quickest and most enjoyable ways of getting to know one another.'

'Quite sure.'

'Pity.'

'Now, if you'd please go.'

'If that's what you really want... Goodnight, Nicola. Sweet dreams.'

'Goodnight,' she replied stiffly.

In the doorway he turned to say, 'Oh, by the way, I'm in the next room along. If you should happen to change your mind, there's a communicating door.'

As every nerve in her body tightened in response to that mocking invitation, the heavy door closed behind him with a slight thud.

Feeling oddly shaky, she wondered, Had Dominic been planning this? Was that the real reason he had given her this particular room? To make it easy?

Trying not to think of him, how close he was, how much she wanted to be with him in spite of everything, she looked around her.

Though it had a wonderfully ornate ceiling, the room was decorated and furnished with relative simplicity. Apart from several comfortable-looking chairs, there was a chest of drawers, a wardrobe, a dressing table, and a carved four-poster bed with a blue brocade canopy.

A quick glance showed that all her clothes had been unpacked and put away, and a short ivory satin nightdress and gown folded tidily and left on the counterpane ready for use.

Beside the four-poster was a bedside table with a state-of-the-art telephone on it. Thoughtfully, her small travel-clock had been placed there, alongside the book she had been reading and her grandmother's jewellery box.

On the far wall there was a pair of long, narrow arched windows, and with a little shock of surprise she heard the sudden vicious squall of rain that beat against them.

Hobbling a little, to protect her bad ankle, she crossed the room to the nearest one and folded back the shutters. The lamps shone on the window glass and made broken reflections of the room behind her in the wash of rain.

As, shielding her eyes, she looked over the dark canal there was a vivid flash of lightning. Its split-second eerie brilliance lit up the black water and the wrought-iron balconies and crumbling stucco of the *palazzo* opposite. It was followed almost immediately by a loud clap of thunder which echoed and re-echoed.

The storm had finally arrived.

While she wasn't afraid of it, the electricity in the air made her feel restless and edgy... As did the frustration caused by refusing to satisfy her newly awakened sexual needs.

There was a door on either side of the room, and she hesitated, wondering which led to the bathroom and which through to Dominic's room.

She felt a bittersweet longing to be in his arms, and if

she opened the wrong one and he was waiting for her she might not have the strength to tear herself away a second time.

And that would only compound the unfortunate picture he had formed of her.

A moment's thought reassured her, however. He had said the next bedroom *along*, so the right-hand door must be the one that led into his room.

There was a big old-fashioned lock on it, but there seemed to be no key, nor was there a bolt.

Still, she knew she had only her own longing to fight. Though Dominic was a red-blooded man, she was convinced that he would make no further move. Having issued the invitation, he would now stand back and leave it to her to decide whether or not to accept.

If only he hadn't got totally the wrong impression of her... But, realising only too well how things must *appear*, she couldn't altogether blame him.

Sighing, she wondered if she would ever be able to convince him that she was totally innocent. Or had fate brought them together only to stand on either side of an abyss that could neither be jumped nor bridged?

It was an unbearable thought.

Turning away from it, she opened the other door and found a large and luxurious bathroom, where her modest towelling robe and toilet bag were waiting.

Doing her utmost to push all her worries aside, at least for the moment, she cleaned her teeth and having removed the bandage from her ankle, showered with care.

Then, after brushing out her long hair, so that it tumbled in a pale silken mass around her shoulders, she donned her nightdress, turned off the main lights and climbed wearily into bed.

Its comfort welcomed her.

Switching off the bedside lamp, she closed her eyes, tired

to the point of exhaustion. It had been a long and wearing day, not only physically but mentally.

There had been the car journey, her first sight of Venice, the visit to Ca' Malvasia... And on top of all that she had run the entire gamut of emotions, going from happiness to despair not once, but twice. So much had happened that there had been no chance to think ahead, but tomorrow she would have to make some crucial decisions.

First and foremost, should she return home or carry on with her holiday?

But even as she asked it that question answered itself. There *might* be something she could do to make Dominic see her in a different light, and while there was still the faintest chance of changing his mind she couldn't bring herself to walk away.

And, recalling what Sandy had said about Brent moving in, she realised that returning to the London flat was no longer an option.

Which meant that when she did go back she would have to find herself some new accommodation, or else stay in a hotel...

The second most important thing was what to do about the Ca' Malvasia... Which reminded her that she had a morning appointment with Signor Mancini to be shown over it. An appointment that she would now have no compunction in cancelling...

Her thoughts growing fuzzy, she yawned...

Almost as soon as sleep claimed her, she began to dream...

She was in Ca' Malvasia, climbing the stairs. Everywhere was dark and silent and somehow menacing. She wanted to turn back but, as was the way of dreams, knew that she had no choice but to go on.

Moving like some wraith, she went through a stone archway and down a bare corridor. Away from the faint light that filtered through the gallery's shuttered windows it was even darker, and she felt her way with one hand on the nearest wall.

Above the faint rasping noise it made she became aware of another stealthy sound.

A chill running through her, she stopped and turned, peering into the gloom, holding her breath while she listened.

There it was again, the merest brush of a footfall. The tiny hairs on the back of her neck rose.

Someone was close at hand, creeping up on her, about to reach out of the darkness and touch her.

Suddenly drenched in icy perspiration, she gave a strangled scream and tried to run.

She had only taken a few stumbling steps when she came up against a solid wall. Heart pounding, sobbing for breath, she scrabbled at it blindly, frantically, feeling for a door. There *had* to be a way through to safety...

CHAPTER SEVEN

ALL at once a door opened, letting light stream in from the room beyond, and a moment later, finding her out of bed, Dominic had gathered her into his arms.

At first, still trapped in the web of panic, she struggled wildly.

Holding her with infinite care, he murmured, 'Gently, gently... It's all right... Everything's all right. It's just a nightmare.'

When she stopped struggling and slumped against him, trembling in every limb, he held her close. He could feel her ribcage heaving and her heart pounding.

Her head cradled against his chest, his mouth buried in her fragrant hair, he continued to murmur soothingly until the harsh sobbing breaths eased and her heartbeat returned to something like normal.

'All right now?' he asked, after a while.

'Yes, I'm all right.' But her voice was muffled and husky, and she continued to tremble.

He stooped and lifted her. 'Then let's get you back to bed.'

As he laid her on the bed and pulled the light covers over her the darkness and terror came crowding back. Cold, despite the heat, and still not fully awake, she clutched at his hand. 'Please don't leave me,' she begged.

'I won't leave you,' he promised.

Having closed the communicating door, he discarded the short silk robe he was wearing and slid in beside her. Then, gathering her to him, he settled her head on his shoulder.

*   *   *

When Nicola stirred and drifted to the surface there was an absence of sound, a quality of stillness, that suggested it was very early morning.

Still more than half-asleep, she was aware of a feeling of warmth and security, a sense of happiness that was all-embracing.

As she lay, little facts began to filter into her consciousness. One of her legs was resting against another hair-roughened leg, there was the weight of an arm across her ribcage, and her cheek was pillowed comfortably on a smoothly muscled chest.

After being alone for so long it was wonderful and, sighing, she nestled closer.

'Good morning.'

She opened heavy lids to find Dominic staring down at her. He was studying her intently, unsmilingly, his grey eyes fixed on her with a look that might have been mistaken for tenderness.

His handsome face was very close and she could see the absurd length of his lashes, the little creases beside his chiselled mouth and the dark stubble adorning his jaw.

As she gazed up at him he met her eyes and smiled into them. Then, putting a finger beneath her chin, he tilted her face so he could more easily kiss her lips.

Helplessly moved by a stirring that was part physical, part emotional, she responded to that kiss, felt not only on her mouth but in every fibre of her being, sweet and disturbing.

He made a little sound in his throat, a mingling of desire and satisfaction, and deepened the kiss.

Instantly she was caught up and carried away by a wave of *need* so powerful that it washed away any hope of resistance.

But it was need on more than one level.

From their very first meeting her feelings for Dominic hadn't been only sexual. He might be proud and arrogant and prejudiced, but she knew deep within her soul that intellectually and emotionally, as well as physically, he was everything she needed and wanted.

And more.

As he kissed her, his demanding, skilful hand moved down to cup and caress her breast through the thin satin of her nightdress.

After a moment he raised his head to say thickly, 'Satin's all well and good, but it's the silk of your skin that I want to touch.'

He began to strip off the unwanted nightdress.

Eager for his touch, she helped him pull the garment over her head and discard it.

Her creamy breasts were small and high and beautifully shaped, with erect dusky-pink nipples that invited his attention.

As soon as he had looked his fill, they got it.

He was a generous lover, and with only his fingers and his mouth he took her to the heights.

Obviously enjoying what was happening as much as she was, he continued to stroke and touch and taste until she thought there could be no further pleasure he could give her.

But then, surprisingly and sweetly inventive, he led her into new discoveries of herself that made her whole being throb and sing with delight.

By the time he lowered himself into the waiting cradle of her hips, sure she was sated, she thought only of him. But at his first strong thrust a spiral of bliss began to build deep inside: a spiral that grew and intensified until it exploded into dazzling fragments of ecstasy.

Though he had given her more pleasure than she had ever thought possible, when it was finally over she found her greatest joy was to cradle his dark head against her breast.

* * *

When Nicola awoke for the second time it was to instant and complete remembrance, and a jumble of warring emotions.

She had meant to sleep alone, and had almost managed it—until circumstances had conspired against her by bringing Dominic to her side.

Feeling her heart pick up speed, she turned her head, only to find that she was alone in the big bed.

Sharp disappointment and cowardly relief mingled. One half of her badly wanted Dominic to be still lying beside her, while the other cringed at the thought of having to face him.

Still recalling all the pleasure that had been lavished on it, her body felt sleek and well satisfied. Utterly content.

Her mind wasn't so happy.

As she lay staring up at the richly embroidered canopy, a sense of failure, of self-condemnation, gnawed at her.

How could she expect Dominic to believe that her actions since they had met had been wholly foreign to her? How could she expect him to believe that her relationship with John had been completely innocent when everything she had done pointed to the contrary?

She sighed deeply. If she told him the simple truth, that she loved him, he would never believe her.

She loved him... Her subconscious had put her feelings for Dominic into words.

She had loved her husband. But with hindsight she could see that her love for Jeff had been a gentle, familiar, one-dimensional emotion that had grown with propinquity and been nurtured by the need to love *someone*.

Whereas the love she felt for Dominic had been practically instantaneous. A strange and powerful three-dimensional emotion that had sprung to life fully grown and taken her over heart and soul before she had been aware of its existence.

Her quiet love for Jeff had been returned in full. But this passionate love she felt for Dominic seemed fated to be unrequited.

Pierced by the painful thought, she sat up.

The room, which overnight had changed from strange to familiar in the way that rooms did after a short acquaintance, was cool and dim. In the air was the scent of lavender, and sunlight slanting obliquely through the shutters made tiger-stripes across the counterpane.

Though it felt early, a glance at the watch she wore on her left wrist showed that it was almost a quarter to twelve, and she had already missed her appointment with Signor Mancini.

At that instant there was a tap at the door.

A shade uncertainly, she called, 'Come in.'

She was taken completely by surprise when Dominic walked in. He was wearing casual trousers and an open-necked shirt, and carrying a silver oblong tray.

'I hope I didn't wake you. I got up to make your breakfast.'

'No,' she said in some confusion. 'I really should have been up long ago. I had an early-morning appointment with Signor Mancini.'

'When I realised you weren't going to make it, I rang him.'

'Thank you.'

'I have Maria's permission to bring you a cup of coffee and a croissant, so long as I do it circumspectly,' he informed her gravely.

With a grin, he added, 'I imagine she thinks you'll be up and fully dressed by now. If she knew you were still in bed and stark naked, she'd have a fit...'

The reminder of her nakedness made Nicola blush and hurriedly pull up the counterpane to cover her breasts.

Dominic sighed. 'While modesty in a woman is seen to be a virtue, it can spoil a man's enjoyment.'

As she blushed to the roots of her hair, he went on, 'Though I must say Maria would approve. She's very proper. She's run the old place with a rod of iron since before I was born.' Ruefully, he added, 'We're all still scared stiff of her.'

The thought of Dominic being scared stiff of any woman, let alone his own housekeeper, made Nicola smile.

Her smile was enchanting. It lit her green eyes, added a breathtaking warmth and charm, transformed her face from merely beautiful to incandescent.

Standing quite still, he feasted his eyes on her. The mass of silky corn-coloured hair that tumbled around her shoulders; the long, slender neck; the smooth creamy line of her collar-bone; the way she had tucked the counterpane beneath her arms to prevent it slipping down...

Flustered by his steady regard, she jerked the counterpane even higher.

Seeing her discomfort, he put the tray supports down and settled it across her knees before coming to sit on the edge of the bed, warning quizzically, 'Don't tell Maria.'

On the tray was a small silver coffee pot, a jug of cream, a bowl of brown sugar, a cup and saucer and, lying on a white damask napkin, a single, perfect red rose.

She stared at it as though spellbound until her gaze was drawn upwards to meet Dominic's.

Grey eyes looked deep into green, conveying a silent message that made her heart swell with happiness. But all he said was, 'The rose is from me.'

'Thank you.' Her voice was husky. 'It's beautiful.'

And it was. Just past the bud stage, the velvety petals were a deep crimson shading to almost black, and the leaves a dark and glossy green.

As she lifted it up to smell its fragrance a sharp thorn pricked her finger.

She gave an involuntary exclamation.

He saw the drop of bright blood welling, and, taking the rose from her hand, tossed it carelessly onto the bedside table. Then, putting her finger in his mouth, he sucked.

Desire kicked low in her stomach and began to form a pool of liquid heat as she remembered the urgent and piercing pleasure of making love with him.

Round a mouthful of finger, he mumbled, 'Can't be too careful with roses.'

'It's quite all right, really,' she told him in a strangled voice.

Letting go of her hand, he said thoughtfully, 'Perhaps I should have made it a hothouse bloom after all...'

She shook her head. 'There's something so sterile, so artificial, about hothouse blooms. I much prefer a garden rose, thorns and all.'

He gave her a strange, almost enquiring look. 'Or maybe a gold brooch in the shape of a rose?'

All her new-found happiness shrivelled and died. 'You mean for services rendered?'

'I wouldn't have put it quite so bluntly. But you're such an absolute joy to make love to that if you *were* looking for a meal-ticket it would be well worth it.'

Feeling as if a cold weight had settled in her stomach, she said, 'As I told you last night, I'm not. Now if you'd please go.'

'Ordering me out is getting to be a habit,' he pointed out mildly.

Flushing, she said, 'I'm sorry. I won't be doing it again. As soon as I'm dressed, I'm leaving.'

He shook his head. 'I'm afraid I can't allow you to leave.'

'You can't make me stay here against my will,' she protested. But, remembering how easily he had dealt with her opposition the previous night, she suddenly wasn't so sure.

'It won't be against your will. If you consider the matter logically, I'm sure you'll come round to my way of thinking. You see, it makes sense from a purely practical point of view. This is the height of the tourist season and every hotel will be booked solid. You'll find it impossible to get any accommodation…'

Nicola was about to tell him she'd chance it, when he carried on evenly, 'But more important is the need to prevent any possible gossip.'

'Gossip?' she echoed blankly.

'News travels fast in such a self-contained community. Venetian society, and especially all my friends, would think it distinctly odd if the person who inherited the *palazzo* wasn't staying there.

'Call it family pride, whatever you like, but the Loredan name is an old and aristocratic one and still highly respected.

'Over the centuries several of the Loredan men became doges and wielded real power. The merest whisper that Sophia Loredan's husband had been foolish enough to leave such a bequest to a young woman the family refused to accept would soon cause a scandal, and that I will not allow.'

'Then I'll move into Ca' Malvasia,' she retorted. 'No one can object to me living there.'

'I can,' he disagreed quietly. 'You see the building was never legally divided. To all intents and purposes Ca' Malvasia is still part of the *palazzo*.'

'What do you mean, "to all intents and purposes"?'

'I mean I could claim it is. If the matter went to court it might take some time to resolve.' With a slight smile, he added, 'It's touch and go who would win in the end, but in the meantime I could certainly prevent you living there.'

He gave her a moment or two to think it over, before going on, 'Now, rather than putting us both to so much trouble, wouldn't it be a great deal easier to simply stay here until you make up your mind what to do with it?'

Already knowing the answer, she asked, 'What do you *want* me to do with it?'

'Sell it back to me.'

'For a song?'

'For the market price.'

'What if I don't want to sell?'

'Then I'll have a very beautiful neighbour.'

'Don't you mean a thorn in your side?'

He gave her a glinting look. 'There's little doubt you *could* be, if you so wished. But I'm rather hoping you won't go down that particular path. It's a great deal more pleasant to be friends...'

With just the slightest touch of menace in his voice, he added, 'And for your own sake, Nicola, I must warn you that I make a very unpleasant enemy to have.'

Yes, she had little doubt that he could be quite ruthless if he felt the need.

A shiver ran down her spine.

He saw that betraying movement, and smiled grimly. 'Now we understand each other, perhaps we can forget any slight unpleasantness and get back on an amicable footing?'

When she failed to answer, he smoothly laid it on the line, 'And while you enjoy your holiday and decide on your future plans you will be a welcome guest at my home.'

'Don't you mean a prisoner?' she asked bitterly.

'How melodramatic,' he mocked. 'Just try to think of the *palazzo* as a hotel.'

'I'm afraid I can't think of it as anything but a prison.'

'Well, at least it's a luxurious prison. Well suited to your preferred lifestyle... And of course it's an "open" one. There used to be dungeons in the old days. Still are, as a matter of fact, but now they're used for storing wine rather than locking up prisoners, so you'll be free to come and go as you wish.'

'But no doubt kept under surveillance?'

'I never do anything that I don't consider is necessary.'

He headed for the door, leaving her to interpret that as she wished.

In the doorway, he turned to say, 'Having dealt with any urgent business, I've decided to take the afternoon off, so I hope you'll join me for lunch on the terrace, at one…'

Though carefully phrased, she recognised it for what it was—a gauntlet thrown down to tempt her.

But before she picked it up she needed time to think…

'That is if your ankle is better…?' he added.

If she said it wasn't, he would no doubt come up and fetch her.

Deciding to play safe, at least for the moment, she assured him coolly, 'I'm sure it will be.'

'Good.' He went out, closing the door quietly behind him.

Feeling as though she'd been put through a wringer, Nicola lifted the silver pot with a shaking hand and poured herself a cup of coffee. She added a little cream and drank it abstractedly while she considered her options, of which there were few. Three at the most.

She could throw in the towel and go home at once.

But that option she immediately ruled out. Though she no longer had any hope of changing Dominic's mind about her, she wasn't going to let him just drive her away.

Her second option was to pick up the gauntlet and try to find somewhere else to stay—she didn't for a moment doubt that if he took the appropriate steps he could prevent her staying at Ca' Malvasia, though surely such a move would risk starting the gossip he was so keen to avoid?—but defying him would mean serious confrontation.

She would be taking a big chance if she called his bluff,

either over the possibility of gossip or him trying to take Ca' Malvasia away from her.

And of course there was always the danger that he wasn't bluffing and that she would end up in the middle of a scandal with nothing. With Dominic as her enemy.

Though, whether he was or not, what was the point of engaging in a long drawn out war of attrition? A war that, with the power Dominic wielded, would almost certainly end in her defeat.

Which left only the third and final option. She would have to bow to the inevitable and stay at the *palazzo*.

It would at least keep open hostility at bay and give her the time she needed to decide what to do.

Already she knew that she didn't want to part with Ca' Malvasia, and if it hadn't been for Dominic she wouldn't even have considered it.

But he wanted it back, intended to have it back, and looking at the matter from his point of view she could understand why...

Somewhere in the distance, a dog barked.

Roused from her thoughts, she glanced at her watch. Half-past twelve. She didn't want to be late for lunch.

If she was to be his 'guest', at least for the next day or so, it would make life a lot easier if she tried to ensure that everything went as smoothly as possible.

Putting aside the tray, she got out of bed, and was pleased to find that her ankle felt almost normal. She was about to head for the bathroom when she noticed the rose lying on the bedside table.

It was still beautiful, but now she looked at it with vastly altered feelings, undecided whether to throw it away or simply leave it there to wilt.

But in spite of the fact that its gift had been just an empty mockery, she couldn't bring herself to do either. Picking it up, she carried it into the bathroom and put it in a glass of water.

When she had showered and cleaned her teeth she brushed out her hair, wincing a little as she touched the bruised area high on her temple. But she had been extremely lucky. It could have been so much worse.

Though it was pleasantly cool inside the shuttered rooms of the *palazzo*, she knew that outside the sun would be baking, so instead of make-up she applied some sunscreen and a touch of pale apricot lipgloss.

Then, after taking her hair up into its usual smooth, gleaming coil, she dressed in a simple sheath and flat-heeled sandals, and at five minutes to one, her defences firmly in place, sallied forth.

Having descended the grand staircase, she was hesitating at the bottom, wondering which of the many doors led outside, when a stocky, silver-haired manservant appeared.

With a stately bow, he said in excellent English, 'The master asked me to be on hand to show you to the terrace… So if you will follow me…?'

'Thank you.'

As she walked in the wake of the black-clad figure she discovered that the *palazzo* was even larger and more imposing than she had first thought. Altered over the centuries, and modernised in parts, it was built in a rectangle around a central courtyard and garden.

Outside there appeared to be no trace of the previous night's storm. The ground was dry, and the air was warm and still and scented with roses. On the steps that led down from the terrace to the garden, several small green lizards were sunning themselves.

In the centre of the paved court was a marble fountain, with water pouring from a tumble of rocks and a trio of long-maned white horses galloping through the spray.

This fountain and the one in the *campo* appeared to have

been designed by the same sculptor, Nicola thought, finding the sound of running water, with its musical splash and gurgle, oddly cooling and refreshing.

Wearing dark glasses, the sun beating down on his head, Dominic was sitting in a lounger glancing through what appeared to be a sheaf of business papers.

Nicola felt the urge to turn and run, but, endeavouring to look calm and collected—which she most definitely was not—she made herself walk towards him.

At her approach he put both the papers and the glasses aside and, every inch the polished host, rose to his feet with a smile.

When she failed to return his smile, he made a point of taking her hand.

Moved as always by his touch, but intent on staying behind her defences and treating him with distant civility, she let her hand stay in his for just a moment before withdrawing it.

His head tilted a little to one side, he studied her silky dress, patterned in subtle shades of green and grey, before remarking, 'You look delightfully cool and fresh... Which in this heat is no mean feat.'

Not knowing how to respond to his unexpected compliment, she found herself saying stiltedly, 'Somehow the fountain makes things seem cooler.'

'When I was quite small, though I knew it was strictly forbidden, I used to climb into it fully clothed and ride on the horses. Much to Maria's horror, I might add. One day when I refused to come out she was forced to wade in after me...'

Amused and intrigued by this glimpse of Dominic as a small and naughty child, Nicola found herself smiling, before it occurred to her that that was precisely why he'd told her the little anecdote.

Part-way along the terrace, where shrubs and vines provided welcome shade from the sun, a buffet table had been set up. It had a centrepiece of fresh flowers and was laid with starched napkins, monogrammed silver and crystal glasses.

Having settled her into a chair, he took a seat opposite and, watching her expressive face, grinned. 'I did tell Maria a *simple* meal, but this is the nearest she can get to a picnic. I think she seriously disapproves of eating in the open air. Now, may I pour you some wine?'

'No, thank you. In this heat I'd prefer water.'

'How sensible of you.' He picked up a tall jug and poured iced water into two lovely glass goblets.

'You must be hungry, as you've had no breakfast, so what will you start with? Something not too heavy? Seafood, perhaps…?'

Throughout lunch, as though his strategy was to disarm her and lure her from behind her defences, he talked lightly, easily, about a variety of subjects.

Determined to follow his lead, she answered in the same vein, and gradually found herself relaxing into the role of welcome guest that he had forced upon her.

By the coffee stage, after a remark Nicola had made about the beauty of the goblets, they had got on to glass-making.

'Glass has been made in Venice for over a thousand years,' Dominic told her. 'The furnaces were originally in the historic centre, but because of the risk of fire they were moved to the island of Murano late in the thirteenth century. There are still quite a few glass factories there, if you would like to see the glass-blowers at work?'

'Oh, yes, I would,' she said eagerly.

'Then, if your ankle isn't paining you at all, we could perhaps go over to Murano this afternoon. Of course these days quite a few of the factories are engaged in making cheap showy stuff for the tourists. However, there are still some real craftsmen about, able to produce the finest work… Things like this, for instance.'

He pointed to the clear, colourless *cristallo* container that held the centrepiece of flowers.

Shaped like a conch shell, and so fine as to be almost invisible, it was an exquisite piece of craftsmanship.

'It's absolutely wonderful,' Nicola said sincerely. 'Is it modern?'

'Yes. I bought it as a wedding gift for my mother and John. I don't think *he* cared for it much, but my mother loved it, and after she died he asked if I'd like to have it back.'

'I can't understand John not liking it. He had an eye for beauty.'

'Obviously.'

Angry with herself for making that incautious remark and providing him with an opening, Nicola bit her lip.

After a moment, he pursued evenly. 'There's something I've been meaning to ask you. As you and John were such close *friends*, why didn't you come to his funeral?'

'He'd been dead for three weeks before I was told about it. I'd been working away.'

Hearing the unmistakable ring of regret and sadness in her voice, Dominic suggested, 'Well, while you're in Venice, if you'd like to see where his remains are buried…?'

Frowning, she said, 'I understand he died in Rome?'

'Yes, he did. But as my mother had expressed a wish that they should lie side by side he was brought back to the family mausoleum on San Michele.'

'I'm so *glad*,' Nicola exclaimed fervently. 'It would have been what *he* wanted too…' Her voice faltered and her almond eyes filled with tears.

Frowning, Dominic queried, 'His death really upset you?'

Blinking away the tears, she took a deep, calming breath. 'Yes. As I've already told you, I was very fond of him.'

'Still, leaving you everything he owned must have made up for a great deal?'

'It didn't make up for losing one of the few people I could call a friend.'

As though trying to make a point, Dominic persevered. 'But surely being named his beneficiary must have been more...shall we say...*rewarding* than merely accepting gifts.'

'I don't know what you mean,' she informed him coldly. 'John never gave me any gifts.'

'None at all?'

'None at all.'

His grey eyes hard as granite, he asked, 'Are you sure about that?'

'Quite sure.' Desperately, she added, 'I would never have taken gifts from him.'

'That's strange, because I have every reason to believe that he gave you a gold ring. A Maschera ring.'

Nicola's face flamed. 'Oh, but he didn't give—'

'Don't bother to deny it. Though Muller was unable to find any trace of it when he searched your cases, I'm quite certain—'

'How dare you have someone search through my things?' she cried furiously. 'You had absolutely no right—'

'I have every right when I'm convinced you have something that doesn't belong to you.'

'So, not satisfied with labelling me a gold-digger, now you're calling me a thief!'

His lips tightened. 'That ring is very precious. I should have kept it safe—'

'So why didn't you?'

'At Mother's funeral I noticed that John was wearing it on a chain around his neck. I should have demanded its return there and then, but he seemed genuinely distraught and I couldn't bring myself to.

'He left Venice the next morning, and when I managed to locate him and ask for it back he refused to part with it. He swore Mother had given it to him on her deathbed—'

'Well, if that's what he says, then surely—'

Disregarding the interruption, Dominic went on with quiet certainty, 'But he was either lying or mistaken. I know for a fact that she would never have done any such thing.'

'What makes you so certain?'

'Because that ring is irreplaceable. It's a family heirloom. After John died it was the first thing we looked for, but there was no trace of it amongst his personal possessions.'

'So you immediately jumped to the conclusion that I must have it?'

'And I was right, wasn't I? Even though you're still trying to deny it.'

'I'm not trying to deny I have it. What I am denying is that John gave it to me—'

'So you're admitting you stole it?'

'I'm admitting nothing of the kind. If you'd only *listen* to me. Let me explain. He didn't *give* me the ring in the way you mean. It was in the packet that Mr Harthill, the solicitor, was keeping for me, along with the keys to Ca' Malvasia.'

'Did you know it belonged to my mother?'

'I knew it had belonged to John's wife.'

With quiet fury, Dominic said, 'He had no right to give it away. Apart from anything else, it's one of the few original Maschera rings still in existence, and that makes it practically priceless.'

CHAPTER EIGHT

'I SHOULD have realised it all came down to money,' Nicola remarked bitterly.

'Are you trying to tell me you didn't know it was worth a fortune?'

'I'm not *trying* to tell you. I *am* telling you. As far as I was concerned, it might well have been simply good costume jewellery. Until now I had no idea of how much it was worth.'

'It isn't just what it's worth in money. That ring has been in the Loredan family since the early seventeen hundreds. For generations it's been passed on to the wife of the eldest son. Or, if there are no sons, to the oldest daughter.'

'I see,' she said slowly.

'But you didn't feel guilty?'

Agitation brought Nicola to her feet, a bright flag of colour flying in each cheek. 'Why should I have felt guilty? I didn't know any of this.'

'Please sit down,' Dominic ordered quietly.

Sinking back into her chair, and only too aware that she sounded both resentful and defensive, she told him, 'All I knew was that the ring had belonged to John's wife and he wanted me to have it—'

She stopped speaking abruptly. Standing a few yards away, in the shadow cast by a thick vine, apparently eavesdropping, was a tall, good-looking young man with black curly hair.

She had thought at first that Dominic was like Jeff, but this man was even more so, and she was unable to take her eyes off him.

Seeing she was looking fixedly over his shoulder, Dominic turned his head. 'What the devil are you doing here?' he demanded curtly.

Unabashed, the younger man gave him a mocking glance and moved out into the sunshine. 'In case you've forgotten, I live here.'

'In case *you've* forgotten, you're supposed to be at an important meeting in Mestre at two o'clock.'

'I didn't forget. I didn't feel like going.'

Watching Dominic's jaw tighten ominously, he added hastily, 'Stomach pains. Been having them for a couple of days. Ever since I ate that lobster...'

'Save the excuses.'

'Look, I've asked one of the secretaries to attend the meeting and take notes...'

Dominic pushed back his chair and rose to his feet, anger in every line of his lean body. 'This meeting was set up to discuss Zitelle's new project. Sending one of the secretaries to take notes just isn't good enough!'

'Oh, Rosa's quick and accurate. She'll include all the salient points and give me a printout.'

'As Rosa happens to be Pietro's secretary she'll no doubt have her own job to do.'

'I'm sure she won't let me down. She's got the hots for me.'

A look of disgust on his face, Dominic said coldly, 'When I entrusted this to you I thought I'd made it clear that we need a personal presence there.'

'But I know next to nothing about Zitelle's new project—'

'You'd know a great deal more if you bothered to attend the meeting.'

'It's a damn sight too hot to be sitting in a boring meeting, especially as I don't feel well.' With a kind of sly defiance, he added, 'And I don't see *you* working.'

'I've been working from home.'

His eyes travelling appreciatively over Nicola, the new-comer remarked, 'Nice work if you can get it.'

'You'll keep a civil tongue in your head,' Dominic ordered sharply.

Then turning to Nicola, he said formally, 'I hope you'll accept my apologies. It's the height of bad manners to quarrel in front of a guest.'

'Oh, I'd hardly call it quarrelling,' the younger man disagreed lightly, 'just a demonstration of brotherly disharmony...'

So this was David. She had already guessed as much by the resemblance, but his remark confirmed it.

Like a small boy showing off, he added, 'And a spot of disharmony isn't to be wondered at when you come to consider how much the head of the house enjoys laying down the law...'

It was plain that David was hell-bent on annoying his brother, and Nicola got the distinct impression that her presence was making him a great deal bolder than he might otherwise have been.

But, his temper leashed, Dominic was once more calmly in control. 'Nicola, may I introduce my brother David? David, this is Mrs Whitney.'

Gazing into her eyes, David took her hand. 'It's a pleasure to meet you, Mrs Whitney...'

He really was a charmer, she thought—and didn't he know it?

'...or may I call you Nicola?'

'Please do,' she said carefully.

'I understand your husband's dead?'

'That's right.' Her voice was steady.

'You're much too young to be a widow. And far too beautiful...'

Still holding her hand, he added deliberately, 'I can quite

see why Dom invited you to stay. Though I must say that in the circumstances I'm surprised you agreed—'

'Are you intending to have lunch?' Dominic broke in abruptly.

'No. I ate at Leonardo's before I came home.'

Only too aware that Dominic was watching, Nicola made a determined effort to withdraw her hand.

Releasing it reluctantly, David smiled at her and carried on speaking as though there'd been no interruption. 'However, I'm glad you did. You'll certainly help to brighten up the old place.'

'I don't expect to be here for long,' she said a shade awkwardly.

'How long is *long*?'

She answered truthfully, 'Just until I have time to decide what to do about…things.'

'You mean selling Ca' Malvasia? Oh, but you mustn't do that. Why not move into the place? Become our neighbour? You've no idea how boring it can be living in—'

Dominic gave him a look that effectively stopped the flow of words; then, speaking into the sudden silence, addressing Nicola, he said formally, 'If you'll excuse me? I must give Bruno Zitelle my apologies and arrange to have someone else attend the meeting.'

Turning to David, he added grimly, 'But first I'd like a word with you.'

Drawing his brother to one side, he began to reprimand him. Though he spoke in an undertone, never once raising his voice, it was obvious that whatever he was saying was more than enough to seriously deflate the younger man.

In no doubt whatsoever which was the stronger of the two, Nicola watched the pair of them, noting the similarities and the differences between them.

They were each over six feet tall, but Dominic was more

strongly built and had a mature width of shoulder the younger man lacked.

Both men were raven-haired, but while Dominic's hair was cut short and tamed David's was an unruly riot of curls.

With less angular features, and blue eyes instead of grey, at first glance David appeared to be much the better-looking of the two.

But a second glance showed that his handsome face was spoilt by a self-indulgent mouth and a weak chin, and he had none of his brother's powerful attraction.

The conversation over, and after a brief glance in Nicola's direction, Dominic went back into the *palazzo*, while, a slight flush lying along his cheekbones, David returned to her side.

Removing his jacket, he tossed it carelessly onto the nearest lounger, and, dropping into a chair, said, 'Phew!'

'Laying down the law?' she asked sympathetically.

'Big time. As far as you're concerned, he's just warned me off so emphatically that, reading between the lines, I'd say he's fallen for you himself... No, on second thoughts, I'd *swear* to it.'

Feeling her face grow hot, she shook her head. 'I'm sure you're wrong. He doesn't even like me. In fact quite the opposite.'

'Then why did he invite you to stay at the *palazzo*?' David asked shrewdly.

Unwilling to go into details, she said, 'I think he wanted me here so he could...keep an eye on me.'

'And no doubt bring pressure to bear to get you to sell Ca' Malvasia?'

'Yes.'

'He does want it back very badly.'

'As he regards it as part of the *palazzo*, that's understandable,' she admitted.

'Will you part with it?' David asked curiously.

'I don't want to, but—'

'Then don't. He can't force you to sell.'

'Probably not. But as things are…'

'Don't let him bulldoze you into doing something you don't want to do. If necessary you should fight him all the way.'

If she hadn't felt the way she did about him, she might well have done. But, as it was, she didn't have the heart to fight.

What was the point? If she won, Dominic would almost certainly hate her… And she couldn't bear to live next door to him knowing he didn't want her there.

Watching the despairing look on her face, David hazarded, 'Afraid you wouldn't win?'

'I'm afraid it might be a hollow victory.'

'Big brother certainly knows how to intimidate people.' He grinned suddenly and admitted, 'When Dom gets really angry he frightens the hell out of me… And today he was livid. After he'd told me to leave you alone, he gave me a tongue-lashing for not being at that meeting, and for what he called "impertinence".'

Dryly, she asked, 'And you don't feel it was deserved?'

He groaned. 'I didn't think *you'd* be on his side.'

'I'm not on anyone's side. But you did go out of your way to aggravate him.'

'I can't seem to help it,' David admitted, with disarming honesty. 'He's so bossy, so arrogant, so damn critical of everything I do. He makes me feel humiliated, puts my back up…'

Nicola felt a quick rush of sympathy. She too had been forced to cope with the bossiness, the arrogance, the feeling of being humiliated…

With a spurt of impatience, he added, 'I wish I didn't have to work for him.'

It was such a relief to forget her own troubles for a bit,

and talk about his, that she found herself asking, 'Are you forced to work for him?'

He said ruefully, reaching to pour himself a glass of wine, 'If I don't work he won't give me an allowance. You see, he holds the purse strings. Though I ought by rights to have money, I can't get my hands on it until I'm thirty. Which is a blasted nuisance. I hate living in a mausoleum like Venice. As soon as I get the chance, I'm off to the States—'

Sounding bitter, he went on, 'But for the moment I'm stuck here without a cent, all because big brother persuaded Mamma that if I got my inheritance too soon I'd fritter it away.'

'*Did* he persuade her? I got the impression that your mother was a lady who made up her own mind about things.'

'Well, whether he persuaded her or she decided for herself, the result's the same. I'll be living like a pauper until I'm thirty…'

Hardly a *pauper*, she thought with a touch of wry amusement. Neither his well-cut suit and silk shirt, nor his hand-made shoes, had come cheap.

'You mentioned an allowance…'

'A mere pittance. And when I took a holiday Dom hadn't sanctioned he threatened to stop it.'

'Couldn't you work for someone else?'

'I tried it once, but the wages were laughable and they expected me to be there five days out of seven.'

'Tough!'

He grinned briefly at the sarcasm, before going on, 'At least while I'm working for DIL Holdings as the boss's brother I get quite a few perks, and when Dom isn't around I can do pretty much as I please.'

Nicola, who was no longer so sure where her sympathies lay, was about to suggest that he really wasn't so hard done by, when he asked, 'What are you doing for the rest of the afternoon?'

'Well, I don't really know…'

'Have you seen much of Venice?'

'No, I only arrived yesterday. Your brother did suggest a visit to Murano, but…'

'You won't see Dom again this side of dinnertime,' David assured her with certainty. 'Work's his god. He'll probably go over to Mestre himself rather than lose Zitelle's good will…'

Seeing Nicola's expression, he added quickly, 'It was the truth, you know. I have been having stomach cramps… Though Dom, who's a hard-hearted devil, obviously didn't believe me.'

Nicola, who hadn't believed him either, said, 'I'm not altogether sure I blame him.'

'I really don't know how someone so beautiful can be so unkind,' David complained sweetly. 'You ought to be all womanly sympathy.'

'I might be if I seriously thought my sympathy was justified.' Then, at his hurt expression, 'Well, it did sound a bit thin.'

'Tell you what,' he said magnanimously, 'I'll forgive the fact that you doubted me if you come out with me this afternoon.'

Reminding herself of her decision to make sure things went smoothly, she shook her head. 'No, I'd better not.'

'Because you don't think Dom would approve?'

'I'm sure he wouldn't.'

'So what if he doesn't? Are you seriously scared of him?'

'Of course I'm not scared of him,' she denied, just a shade too hastily, and seeing David's derisory grin gave way to the temptation to add, 'But I thought *you* were.'

'Only when he's around.'

Feeling a sense of camaraderie, and disarmed by the self-mockery, she said seriously, 'But you must know as well as I do that it would be asking for trouble…'

'We're free agents. To hell with him. In any case, how would he know?'

'If he came back and found both of us gone…'

'He won't be back. Once he's working, everything else gets pushed on one side… Surely you don't want to just sit here for the rest of the afternoon?'

With all of Venice on the doorstep, she didn't. Suddenly impatient, tired of inactivity, she wanted to get out and about.

If Dominic had said anything about returning, had asked her to wait for him… But he hadn't.

Seeing her waver, David urged, 'Oh, come on… You're not a prisoner, and we'll be back before he's even missed us.'

'Well perhaps for just an hour or so.'

'That's my girl!' he cried triumphantly.

Suddenly remembering, she said, 'But didn't you have stomach pains?'

'They're much better…'

'How convenient.'

'It's quite true that I *did* have them, so don't look so stern and accusing… Now, do you need to do anything before we start?'

'Just slip upstairs for my bag. I may need some more sunscreen.'

'You're in the east wing, presumably?'

'Yes.'

'Which room?'

As she hesitated, he hazarded with a sly grin, 'I bet Dom gave you the room next to his.'

Noting the confusion she was unable to hide, he added with a slight touch of malice, 'I must say I don't blame him. A communicating door comes in very handy.'

Then, hastily, 'There's no need to be cross. I'm only joking… Now, if you go up by the back stairs it'll save time, and you'll be less likely to meet anyone.'

'I don't know where the back stairs are.'

'Come on, I'll show you.' Picking up his jacket, he seized her hand and hurried her down the steps and across the courtyard to a small door at the rear of the house.

It opened into what were clearly servants' quarters, with kitchens and storerooms and a veritable maze of stone passages. Through another door was a flagged area with a flight of stone steps leading up to an archway.

Pointing upwards, David said, 'If you go through the archway and turn left, there's a corridor that leads straight to the east wing. It should only take you a minute or so. I'll wait for you here…'

Just in case we're seen together, hung on the air unspoken.

Feeling distinctly nervous, almost guilty, Nicola followed his instructions and came out practically opposite the door she now recognised as her own.

Once inside her room she breathed a sigh of relief. But it was absurd to feel guilty, she told herself firmly. It wasn't as if she was doing anything wrong.

Dominic might have warned his brother to stay away from her, but she and David were grown adults—and if, tired of being dictated to, he *wanted* to risk taking her out for an hour or two…

Ignoring the voice of common sense that warned her she shouldn't be a party to it, Nicola opened her shoulder bag and dropped a tube of sunscreen and some tissues into it.

She was just closing it again when, with a sudden shock, she recalled what Dominic had told her about Sophia's ring being priceless.

Unzipping the small compartment at the back, she took

out the soft leather pouch and put it into her grandmother's jewellery box.

It should be safe enough there for the time being.

Shutting the door quietly behind her, she hurried back the way she had come, her heart beating ridiculously fast.

David was waiting where she had left him. 'See anyone?' he asked.

She shook her head. 'Not a soul.'

'Good. I've got a boat waiting for us. This way.' He crossed to a stout oak door with an iron grille. Even before he drew back the bolts she could hear the surge and slap of water against stone.

The door gave access to a short flight of worn steps and a landing stage.

'This isn't the way Dominic took me last night.' She spoke the thought aloud.

'No, that would have been the main entrance. This is the tradesmen's,' he added with a grin.

Both the huge wooden boat-house doors were closed, but a narrow side door led to an outside landing stage where, to her surprise, a black steel-prowed gondola was waiting.

The gondolier, dressed in a red-striped T-shirt and a straw hat with a red ribbon, helped Nicola in while David followed on her heels.

As soon as they were settled side by side on the cushioned seat the gondola drew away.

Watching the boatman ply the long oar with marvellous dexterity, she remarked, 'How exciting. I must admit I hadn't expected a gondola.'

'I daren't take one of the motorboats in case Dominic misses it,' David explained. 'And Giorgio can come and go much more quietly than a water-taxi. With a bit of luck no one will realise we've gone.'

'I take it you often use this method of escape?' she asked lightly.

'Yes, I do,' he admitted with cheerful unconcern. 'It saves an awful lot of trouble and tiresome explanations. Being the younger son is a terrible trial… But we're out to enjoy ourselves, so I vote we forget our problems for a while…'

Only too happy to follow his lead, she relaxed and began to enjoy the strange movement of the gondola, which dipped and curtsied in response to the gondolier's single oar.

It was mid-afternoon and the sun was riding high in the sky. Apart from some red-faced, perspiring tourists there were few people about. Most Venetians, it seemed, had retired indoors to escape the sweltering heat.

Leaving Rio Cavalli, and moving from sunlight to shade, they threaded their way through a network of waterways, passing under bridges where the water was dark green and the shadows quiet and deep.

After a while Nicola became aware of the varied smells of the city: fruit, flowers, ground coffee, bread being baked, the sweet, heady scent of wine and spices… And all the time the splash and ripple of water…

She felt a sudden poignant sadness. If only she had been discovering this most picturesque and romantic of cities with Dominic beside her…

'This will do fine, Giorgio. We'll walk from here.' David's voice broke into her thoughts.

A moment later they drew into a gondola park where several of the gondoliers, their straw hats tipped over their faces, were taking a siesta.

When Nicola had been helped out a roll of lira changed hands, and after a low-toned conversation with their boatman David joined her on the *fondamenta*.

As the sun beat down mercilessly the stones they were standing on threw back an oven heat.

His jacket over his arm, perspiration shining on his forehead, he said, 'It's a damn sight too hot for walking about sightseeing… Tell you what, why don't we take a dip instead?'

'A dip?' she echoed.

'If we go over to the Lido we can relax under a beach umbrella and go for a swim.'

'That sounds wonderful… But we haven't got swimwear or towels or changing facilities—'

'That's just where you're wrong. For convenience, I use part of my allowance to keep a permanent room at the Trans Luxor. An arrangement that big brother knows nothing about. Come on.'

Taking her hand, he led her along the *fondamenta* to what she presumed was the Venetian equivalent of a taxi rank, and in a moment they were speeding towards the long, narrow strip of land that formed the Lido.

Once on the island, Nicola was surprised to find that, unlike Venice, there were busy roads with cars and buses and taxis.

David hailed a taxi for the short drive to the hotel, which was a dazzling white building shaded by trees. Inside it was cool and dim and absolutely deserted, except for a pretty young blonde behind the reception desk.

As they crossed the marble-floored lobby David remarked casually, 'Last time one of my girlfriends was here she left her swimsuit in my room…'

Suddenly realising exactly what he'd meant by *convenience*, Nicola wondered whether she'd been wise to come. But it was too late now. Having got this far, she could hardly walk out.

'Gina's just about your size, if you'd like to borrow it?'

Far from enamoured with the idea, Nicola was about to politely refuse when, indicating a small boutique just off the main lobby, he added, 'Or if you'd prefer to have your own you could choose one while I pick up the key.'

By the time he had picked up the key, which involved a

lengthy flirtation and a great deal of giggling on the part of the blonde receptionist, Nicola had selected and paid for a modest black swimsuit.

His ground-floor room was large and well-furnished, with French doors that opened on to the cool greenery of the gardens. Beyond was a private beach bright with umbrella-shaded loungers.

A room like this must cost a great deal to rent on a permanent basis, Nicola thought, deciding that his allowance couldn't be the mere pittance he'd described it as being.

As soon as the door had closed behind them he hung his jacket over the back of a chair and, having drawn the many-layered muslin curtains, began to unbutton his shirt.

'Perhaps I could change in the bathroom?' she suggested evenly.

Indicating a door to the right, he agreed with a mocking grin, 'By all means, if you're feeling particularly modest.'

Refusing to rise to the bait, she went, bolting the door after her just to be on the safe side.

The swimsuit, which fitted her to perfection, was nowhere near as decorous as it had seemed, the legs being cut high and the bust low. She stood for a few seconds trying to adjust it, before giving up the struggle.

As well as the white bath towels there was a pile of coloured beach towels, and after selecting a couple she ventured out, to be greeted by a low, appreciative whistle.

Dressed in red swimming trunks, and sporting what seemed to be an all-over tan, David looked both macho and sexy, and she could quite understand what women saw in him.

But as far as *she* was concerned, measured against Dominic's powerful physique and virile attraction, his brother couldn't compete. The sight of him failed to raise her pulse-rate one iota.

With a suggestive glance at the bed, he said, 'I thought you might fancy a little siesta first?'

'No, thanks.'

'Why not?' he sounded genuinely surprised. Then, as though just stating a fact, he added, 'A lot of women find me irresistible.'

'I believe you. I just don't happen to be one of them.'

'Go on, don't fight it,' he urged.

'I don't need to. To put it bluntly, I find you eminently resistible.'

'You certainly know how to hurt a man's feelings,' he complained with mock indignation.

Liking him for the way he'd taken her rejection in such good part, she said, 'But I do think you're nice.'

Perking up, he suggested, 'If you'd like me to show you just how nice I can be—'

'I wouldn't.'

'We don't have to go for a swim just yet,' he persisted. 'It'll be cooler in an hour or so's time, and there'll be less people.'

'I expect to be back at the *palazzo* in an hour or so's time,' she informed him crisply.

He sighed. 'Then I suppose we'd better get moving.'

The Adriatic was a pale, clear green and refreshingly cool, while the fine sandy beach was clean and golden and shelved gently.

Though most of the loungers were occupied they managed to find two free ones side by side. Enjoying the holiday atmosphere, the pleasure that sun, sea, and sand could bring, they alternately swam and stretched out in the shade, sometimes in companionable silence, sometimes talking idly.

Waking from a doze, and glancing around, Nicola realised that quite a lot of the loungers were empty.

'What time is it?'

'No idea,' David said idly, his eyes still closed.

'I'm sure it must be getting on. We ought to be starting back.' Jumping to her feet, she gathered up her towel and sunscreen.

Reluctantly he followed suit, and led the way through the tree-shaded gardens back to his room. As he unlocked the French doors he offered, 'You can have the bathroom first. Unless you'd like to share a shower?'

'This is no time for joking,' she said severely.

'What makes you think I'm joking?'

She sighed. 'You're incorrigible.'

With a grin he assured her, 'It's part of my charm.'

Going through to the bathroom, she stripped off her swimsuit. Her hair felt sticky with the salt water, and, taking out the pins, she reached for the shampoo.

As soon as she had showered and blowdried her hair, she pulled on her clothes and went back to the bedroom, her hair still loose around her shoulders.

'It's all yours.' Then catching sight of the expression on David's face, she asked sharply, 'What's wrong?'

'Have you seen the time?'

'No, I left my watch in my bag.'

'Take a look.'

With a sudden sense of doom she reached for her bag, which she'd left on a low chest, and felt for her watch.

Staring at the gold hands on the black face, she protested stupidly, 'No, it can't be six-thirty!'

'I'm afraid it is. We've blown it. There's no way we can get home before Dom. In fact, unless we're lucky, we won't be back in time for dinner.'

'Oh, Lord,' she exclaimed in dismay.

Gathering up his clothes, he said, 'Look, while I shower, I'll try to decide what to do.'

'What *can* we do?'

'I'll let you know when I've had a minute to think.' He disappeared into the bathroom, closing the door behind him.

Finding her small brush, Nicola was about to put up her hair when she realised she'd left her pins in the bathroom.

David returned quite quickly, fully dressed, his blue eyes bright, his damp hair clinging to his skull in tight black curls.

'Well?' she asked, without much hope.

'As far as I can see we've only two options. We either go straight back and brazen it out—but I tell you now I'm not much for that course of action; it'll mean being in the doghouse for weeks—or we play it cool.'

'What do you mean by play it cool?'

'Presumably by now Dom will know we're both missing. But he can't be sure we're together. We could have gone out quite independently... Now, my suggestion is this. We don't rush back. In fact we wait until everyone's in bed...'

'Oh, but—'

'We can have a meal out, see a little of Venice by night, then get a gondola back and slip in separately. If we go straight up to our rooms no one need ever know we've been together. Then, if we meet in the morning we greet each other like virtual strangers...'

'But won't it mean telling an awful lot of lies?' she asked unhappily.

'Why should it? If Dom asks me I'll tell him I've been over to the Lido... If he questions you, don't mention the Lido, simply say you've been sightseeing.'

'What if it doesn't work?'

He shrugged. '*If* it doesn't, though there's a good chance that it will, we might as well be hung for sheep as lambs... What do you say?'

She hesitated, disliking the idea of having to lie, even by omission. But she was at least partly to blame. If she hadn't been stupid enough to agree to go out with David none of this would have happened.

And if Dominic *did* discover they'd been together, after he'd warned his brother off, David was going to be the one to suffer the consequences. So if there was a sporting chance of saving the day...

'All right,' she agreed.

'That's my girl!'

CHAPTER NINE

DESPITE her unease, the return journey to Venice by water-taxi was an experience Nicola wouldn't have missed for worlds.

The air was golden and pellucid, and sun sparkled and danced on the lagoon. At David's urging she had left her hair down, and a warm breeze played with the heavy silken mass, blowing curly tendrils across her cheeks.

In the distance the historic centre, with its bridges and bell towers, its temples and palaces, lay like some magnificent backdrop, serene and enchanted against a deep blue sky.

'Isn't it *wonderful*?' she said over the noise of the engine.

'Most people think so.' David sounded indifferent.

Glancing at him, she saw he was completely unmoved by the beauty of the city.

'I suppose, having lived here all my life, I'm used to it,' he added.

Dominic was used to it, but as far as *he* was concerned Venice still hadn't lost either its loveliness or its fascination...

'One thing it does have,' David pursued after a moment, 'are some first-class restaurants. I thought we'd eat at Il Faraone, which is one of the best. They know me there, so we'll have no difficulty getting a table, and if we disembark at Accademia, it's quite close.'

Nicola's ankle had started to swell and stiffen up again, and putting her weight on it had become painful, so she was pleased not to have too far to go.

After disembarking near the Accademia Bridge and walk-

147

ing a little way, they turned into a narrow *calle* that lay in deep shadow.

They were part-way down it when some distance ahead a man coming towards them paused in the shadows to light a cigarette. The flare of the match briefly illuminated a thin, swarthy face with a hooked nose.

Seizing her arm in a vice-like grip, David swung on his heel and headed back the way they'd come.

Nicola felt a tingle of apprehension, sensing something sinister in the little incident. But perhaps she was just being over-imaginative? It could be simply that he had taken a wrong turning.

Though as he appeared to frequent Il Faraone that seemed somewhat unlikely.

A swift glance at his face only served to confirm her suspicion that something was wrong. 'David...' she began.

'It's all right,' he assured her. 'There's no problem. It was just someone I didn't want to run into. This way is just as quick.'

In spite of his attempt to shrug it off she could tell he was rattled. But, reminding herself that it was no business of hers, she said nothing further.

As she might have expected, Il Faraone was elite and stylish, with a well-dressed clientele and a striking Egyptian decor. When David had been greeted by name and made welcome they were shown to one of the best tables.

His smile slightly reckless, he ordered champagne, and when it arrived drank the first glass as though it were lemonade.

The menu was so large and varied that, after glancing through it twice, Nicola sought his advice on what Italian dish to try.

He answered abstractedly, as though his mind was on other things, and they were halfway through the meal before he seemed able to shrug off whatever was bugging him and give her his full attention.

Then, studying her face, he said thoughtfully, 'Apart from the fact that you're beautiful, I know hardly anything about you. Tell me about yourself.'

A little uncomfortably, she asked, 'What would you like to know?'

'What do you do? Or rather what *did* you do before you became a rich woman?'

Ignoring the rather snide way the question was phrased, she told him levelly, 'I'm a conference organiser for Westlake Business Solutions.'

'Was that how you met John?'

'Yes.'

'Did you live with him?'

'No. Nor did I persuade him to leave me his money.'

'I rather thought not. You don't seem to be the gold-digger type.'

He sounded sincere, and, her green eyes suddenly misty, she said, 'Thank you for that.'

'Did he love you?'

'No. He still loved your mother. We were just friends. We hadn't really known each other very long.'

'So why did he leave you everything he had?'

'I'm still not sure. Possibly because he didn't get on with—' She stopped speaking abruptly.

'The rest of the family?' David supplied. Then judiciously, 'Can't say I blame him, personally. Apart from Mamma, nobody else really accepted him, and he must have known it. Though leaving you the Maschera ring was really getting his own back with a vengeance...'

So David *had* been eavesdropping.

'Just for curiosity, have you decided whether or not to let Dom have it back?'

'There's been no time to think about it... I just wish it wasn't *worth* so much,' she burst out raggedly

Curiously, he asked, 'Then you really didn't know how valuable it was?'

'Of course I didn't. I'd hardly have been carrying it around with me if I had.'

'If you were carrying it with you, why didn't Dom's detective find it? I gather he searched your cases.'

'It was in my handbag,' she admitted.

David gave a long, low whistle. 'So you were *literally* carrying it around with you. It's just as well big brother doesn't know that. He'd have a heart attack... Though of course Mamma always wore it,' he continued thoughtfully, 'and no one queried how safe that was.'

Eyeing Nicola's bag, he raised an eyebrow. 'I suppose you're not still...?'

'No,' she said hastily. 'I left it in my room.'

'Safely hidden?'

'I put it in my grandmother's jewellery box.'

He nodded, before commenting with a certain degree of satisfaction, 'I must say Dom hasn't had it all his own way lately. What with being deprived of the ring, and Ca' Malvasia...'

'Not to mention the money.' She failed to hide her bitterness.

'I think the money's the least of his concerns. The lucky devil already has enough. But he does badly want the other two. The woman he's going to marry—'

'He's going to be married?' Even to herself, her voice sounded shocked, impeded.

'Ah!' David exclaimed. 'You're surprised because of what I said earlier, about him having fallen for you?'

Nicola took a deep, steadying breath, and remarked as lightly as possible, 'Well, it just goes to prove you're wrong.'

'Not at all. Until he and Carla are married he'll be allowed his little indulgences, so long as he's discreet and the Ferrinis don't get to hear of it.'

'When...?' She faltered, then went on, 'When are they going to be married?'

'So far as I'm aware they haven't yet set a date.'

Knowing she was just torturing herself, but unable to stop, she asked, 'How long have they known each other?'

'Practically all their lives. Though Carla's quite a bit younger than Dom—more my age. They've been unofficially engaged for over a year. But for some reason, though he admits it's high time he settled down and produced an heir, Dom has been dragging his feet.

'I can't understand why. I wouldn't have done. Carla's a beautiful girl, and the Ferrinis, who were close friends of Mamma's, must be amongst the wealthiest families in Venice. There's also a branch of the family in New York, and they're not short of a dollar or two...'

He sighed. 'If you do decide to let Dom have the ring back I expect it will help to spur him on...'

Her heart like lead, Nicola said, 'I don't see what else I can do. I'd feel bad knowing not only how much it's worth but about the tradition.'

'I must admit I don't see the point of keeping up all these old traditions.' David sounded bored. 'Though Dom is pretty keen on it. He's always seemed to be in tune with the past...

'Whereas Carla's a thoroughly modern girl and probably doesn't care two hoots about the ring. But having Ca' Malvasia back would almost certainly make a difference.'

'You don't mean they'd live there?'

'No, but Carla's mother would. It's already been discussed. Signora Ferrini, who has been recently widowed, would like to sell the Ferrini family home, a huge crumbling place on the Giudecca, and be close to her only daughter.

Dom has already agreed that she could live with them in the *palazzo*, but she wants to keep her independence. If she was able to have Ca' Malvasia it would be ideal.'

Her despair complete, Nicola said, 'No wonder he wants it back so badly.'

'Well, in my opinion you'd be a fool to let him have it.' Then, as though sensing how low she felt, 'But let's forget about Dom and go and paint the town... What about a spot of dancing?'

'That would be lovely,' she said as brightly as possible, 'but I don't think I can. You see I sprained my ankle yesterday, and it's starting to play up again.'

'Which means no walking either?'

'Well, not too much,' she admitted.

'In that case I know the ideal way to spend the rest of the evening. We'll go to the Club Nove. We can sit and have a bottle of champagne while we enjoy the floor show... Oh, just a word of warning. Don't ever mention this to Dom.'

After taking them through a network of back canals, the water-taxi dropped them by a short flight of water-lapped steps which led into a narrow alleyway between high brick walls.

The alley gave on to Campo Mandolo, a rather grand square which, with several bars and open-air restaurants, appeared to be a venue for Venetian night-life.

On the right of the *campo* was a restaurant with a large group of people eating outside at tables set beneath a green and gold awning. Judging by the cake it was a birthday celebration, and there was much talk and laughter and clinking of wine bottles.

By the side of the restaurant was a black studded door with a metal grille. There was no name on it, and nothing to indicate it was a club.

Reaching up, David tugged at the old-fashioned bell-pull.

A face appeared at the grille, and after a moment's silent scrutiny the door was opened by a burly man in evening dress.

Leaning towards him, David said something Nicola didn't catch.

'What about her?' the man asked.

'This is Signora Whitney. She's all right. I'll vouch for her.'

The man nodded, and they were ushered inside and the door closed behind them.

Nicola found herself standing in a bare foyer, with a marble staircase leading upwards. As the man disappeared into a small cubicle David said, 'This way,' and led her up the stairs.

At the top of the stairs was another door with a grille. He rapped briefly with his knuckles, and once more they were silently inspected.

Nothing was said, but the door opened and they were ushered into a large room with luxurious ivory and gold decor and crystal chandeliers. At the far end was a dais with a black baby grand piano.

In front of the dais was a highly polished dance floor the size of a postage stamp, around which were scattered a dozen or so tables.

An elegantly dressed hostess appeared at David's elbow, and with a smile showed them to one of the few unoccupied tables.

She was followed almost immediately by a wine waiter with a bottle of champagne in an ice-bucket and two long-stemmed glasses. Easing out the cork with a nicely controlled pop, the waiter poured the smoking wine before moving away on silent feet.

Nicola got the impression that champagne was part of the usual routine.

Glancing around her curiously, she saw that some of the clientele wore evening clothes, while others were more casually dressed, but they all seemed to have one thing in common—money.

Leaning towards her, David said in her ear, 'Good timing. The floor show's just about to start.'

Sipping champagne, they sat and watched an extremely good show which included a brilliant illusionist and a Frank Sinatra look-alike.

After perhaps an hour, when the pianist was accompanying a husky-voiced blues singer wearing a gold-lamé dress, David began to get restive.

'Let's go through and get a bit of the action.'

'A bit of the action?' Nicola echoed uncertainly, as he pulled back her chair.

He grinned. 'There's no need to look so wary. I only meant a few rolls of the dice.'

So this was a *gambling* club. That explained the rather strange mode of entry.

Recalling his injunction not to tell Dominic, and feeling distinctly uneasy, she said, 'I'm sure this isn't wise. I really think we should go.'

'Don't be such a spoilsport,' he chided her. 'It's only a bit of fun, for goodness' sake. Look, I promise we won't stay long…'

Seeing she was unconvinced, he pulled a mobile phone from his pocket, 'If it makes you any happier I'll call Giorgio and ask him to pick us up in half an hour or so.'

He was clearly determined, and, unwilling to make a fuss, she waited while he had a brief word with the boatman, then reluctantly allowed herself to be shepherded into a side room.

Windowless, and brightly lit by harsh neon lighting, it was as large as the other room, but stark and businesslike, with nothing to distract the gamblers from their game.

There were quite a lot of tables—some set up for baccarat, some for dice games, others for roulette. Most of them were busy.

As they approached one of the tables a seat became vacant. Pushing her into it, David had a quiet word with the banker and was given a pile of pink plastic chips in exchange for what appeared to be an IOU.

On edge and anxious, she watched as he picked up and rattled the dice. 'I really need to win, so keep your fingers crossed.'

'Oh, I *will*,' she said fervently.

Fascinated in spite of herself, she watched as he began to roll the dice with a devil-may-care air quite at odds with the seriousness displayed by most of the gamblers.

Almost immediately he hit a winning streak. From then on it seemed he could do no wrong. 'You've brought me luck,' he said jubilantly, as he threw a double six.

'I'm glad,' she said. Then, urgently, 'Can we go now?'

'While I'm winning?' he sounded amazed.

'Surely that's the time to stop? Please, David. It's getting very late.'

Seeing she was really anxious, he said, 'Just another few rolls, then I'll pack it in.'

But, as though Lady Luck had suddenly withdrawn her favours, he lost on the next roll, and after one more win began to lose steadily.

No longer able to look, Nicola sat with her hands clenched until the banker finally called a halt.

Taking out a pen, David began to plead for a further chance to win back what he'd lost, but to Nicola's great relief the banker was adamant. There was to be no further credit.

His face set, David turned away, and they left the club in a brooding silence.

Everywhere was in darkness now, the bars and restaurant closed, tables and chairs piled together beneath the awnings.

They had crossed the deserted *campo* and were about to turn down the alley, which was unlit, when two men stepped out, barring their way. Both appeared to be brawny, but one was appreciably taller than the other.

'Before you go, we'd like a word with you.'

In the gloom Nicola could see neither of their faces clearly, but their menacing attitude brought a distinct chill of fear.

'Can't you make it some other time?' David asked with a bravado that almost came off. 'As you can see, I have a lady with me.'

The spokesman, who was the taller of the two, said, 'I'm sure she won't mind waiting just a couple of minutes.'

Closing in on David, they hustled him down the alleyway.

If they showed any sign of harming him she'd have to scream, Nicola thought desperately. But all she could hear was the low murmur of voices. A few snatches of conversation in disjointed sentences.

'Why not talk to me at the club…?'

'…disturb the other clientele. So what about it?'

'As soon as I can…'

'You shouldn't have been allowed to get in any deeper. Angelo's not pleased…'

'…pay, I promise…'

'How soon?'

'Another few days…worth his while…'

'He said tomorrow. No later than three o'clock.'

'I'll try, but I—'

'You'll have to do better than try. Angelo's getting impatient.'

They seemed to be returning, and Nicola heard the last few sentences more plainly.

'Remember what happened to the last man Angelo got impatient with.'

'What good would that do?' David sounded scared.

'It might serve as a lesson to others who run up debts when they haven't got the money.'

'But I *have* got the money,' he said desperately. 'Angelo knows that. I just can't get my hands on it at the moment.'

'Then you'd better find some other way to pay…and before three o'clock tomorrow.'

Emerging from the alley, the two men melted into the darkness, leaving David standing alone.

Mingled with her relief that they hadn't harmed him was a very real anxiety. There seemed little doubt that he was up to his neck in trouble.

As she rejoined him, he said with a jauntiness she was forced to admire, 'Sorry about that. Just two rather impetuous friends of mine.'

'Friends' was the last word she would have used, Nicola thought, but he seemed less alarmed by them than by the man he'd avoided earlier.

When they reached the end of the alleyway David gave a sigh of relief to find Giorgio's gondola was drawn up by the steps.

Without a word being spoken Nicola was handed in, and in a moment or two they were threading their way through the dark canals.

They approached the *palazzo* as silently as they'd left it, only the faint creak of the oar and the splash of water to give away their presence.

At the landing-stage David had a whispered conversation with the boatman before a roll of notes changed hands.

Then, putting his lips to Nicola's ear, he said softly, 'I'll go in first, to make sure the coast's clear. Just in case there's a problem give me ten minutes before you follow. Giorgio will tell you when the time's up. Be sure to bolt the door behind you, and use the back stairs like you did before. Once we're both safely in our own rooms no one can swear we've been out together.'

He gave her hand a quick squeeze. 'With a bit of luck we're home and dry.'

To Nicola, sitting waiting in the darkness as the seconds crept by and a balmy night breeze lifted her hair, ten minutes seemed an age. She could see the faint greenish glow of Giorgio's luminous wristwatch without being able to tell the time.

Silent and aloof, the boatman stood like a statue, plying his long oar to keep the gondola steady while the water slopped a little, like a cup of black coffee in an unsteady hand.

When he finally turned his head and gave her a brief nod, she whispered, *'Grazie,'* and allowed herself to be helped onto the landing-stage.

He was drawing away before she had let herself in.

Closing the door quietly behind her, she struggled to push home the stout bolts. Despite her care, both of them grated. In the silence the noise seemed terribly loud, and she stood for a moment, her heart in her mouth.

Then, plucking up courage, she climbed the dimly lit stairs and tiptoed along the corridor. The whole place appeared to be fast asleep, but she held her breath until she had reached her room and slipped inside.

She was endeavouring to close the heavy door quietly when, in the darkness, she misjudged the distance and it shut with a distinct thud.

As she stood there, frozen, the communicating door was thrown open, letting in a flood of light.

Dominic stood in the doorway wearing a dark silk dressing gown. Though his black hair was ruffled, she got the distinct impression that he hadn't yet been to bed.

'Where have you been?' he demanded.

His back was to the light and she couldn't see his face clearly, but there wasn't the slightest doubt that he was *furious*.

'Out.' In spite of all her efforts her voice shook a little.

Taking in the dress and sandals, the shoulder bag and the silken wind-blown hair, he said, 'That's obvious. And it's equally obvious that you've only just returned.'

'Yes,' she admitted.

'Come in here,' he ordered curtly. 'I want to talk to you.'

'Please, Dominic, can't it wait until morning?'

'No, it can't.'

Desperate to postpone the confrontation, she pleaded, 'But I'm tired and my ankle hurts.'

'That I can well believe,' he announced grimly. 'But you have some explaining to do, and I've no intention of letting you stand on the opposite side of the room while you do it, so come along.'

Knowing full well Dominic was capable of sweeping her up and carrying her across the room, Nicola dropped her bag on a chair and reluctantly moved towards him.

He stepped aside to allow her to pass.

Seeing his set face, and suddenly scared stiff of his anger, she hung back.

Seizing her wrist, he drew her inside and closed the door behind her.

She had somehow expected his room to be grand and imposing, but, agitated as she was, she was struck by the simplicity of the off-white walls, the plainness of the furniture. The only thing to echo his wealth and power as the head of the house was a magnificent four-poster with a scarlet and gold canopy.

'Sit down.'

'I'd rather stand.'

'Will you stop behaving like a stubborn little fool and do

as I say?' Though he still hadn't raised his voice, it cracked like a whip.

She sank down in the nearest chair.

Remaining standing, he told her, 'As soon as I'd arranged for someone else to take David's place at the meeting, and made my apologies to Bruno Zitelle, I came back, expecting to take you over to Murano, only to find you'd disappeared.'

'I—I'm sorry,' she stammered. 'But you didn't say you'd be coming back, and David thought—' Realising it was unwise to involve David, she broke off abruptly.

'What *did* David think?'

Carefully, she answered, 'Only that if you once got involved with work it was unlikely you'd be back. He said you might even go over to Mestre yourself, so I decided that rather than just sit there I'd go out for a little while—'

'But it wasn't "a little while". You've been out for hours. When dinnertime came and there was still no sign of you I began to think you'd…'

Though he failed to complete the sentence, she knew exactly what he'd been about to say. 'Gone? Left Venice for good?'

'It did cross my mind,' he admitted.

Though his words were almost casual, she was suddenly quite certain that he'd been *afraid* that she'd gone, that it had *mattered* to him.

For a moment her heart lifted.

Then with a pang she realised that it hadn't been *her* that had mattered, but the fact that she had the Maschera ring.

Sighing, she asked, 'So how did you know I hadn't gone for good?'

'I went up to your room and discovered your belongings were all still there. That reassured me for a while, but when you still failed to return I began to get seriously concerned about you.'

'Well, I'm sorry if you were concerned.' Deciding to fight

back, she added, 'But as you yourself said it was an "open" prison I could see no harm in going out to do some sight-seeing.'

'*Sightseeing*? Have you any idea what time it is?'

'Well, I know it's late but—'

'It's nearly half-past two.'

'Oh...'

'Anything might have happened to you!' With a kind of raging calm, he demanded, 'How could you be so foolish as to go roaming around Venice alone until the early hours of the morning?'

'But I wasn't...' Naturally honest, she made a very poor liar, and, realising she'd almost given David away, she broke off in confusion.

Dominic's eyes narrowed. 'Alone?'

'Roaming around. Quite a lot of the time I was sitting down because of my ankle.'

'Where were you "sitting down" until two o'clock in the morning?'

'I can't remember the name of the place...' Hoping she wasn't giving away too much, she added, 'I had a drink there, then stayed to watch the floor show.'

Her inquisitor changed ground with an abruptness that threw her. 'How did you get in and out of the *palazzo*?'

'I—I don't know what you mean.'

'It's a perfectly simple question.'

When, unsure what to say, she stayed silent, he asked, 'Did you leave and return by the main entrance?'

Guessing that the main entrance would have been locked and bolted before the servants went to bed, she stammered, 'W-well no.'

'So which entrance *did* you use?'

'I went and returned by boat.'

'I see... But not the way I took you last night.'

It was a statement, not a question, and, afraid of putting her foot in it, she once again remained silent.

'So who told you about the tradesmen's entrance?'

Trapped, she cried, 'I refuse to answer any more questions. As a guest here I've every right to come and go as I please, without being interrogated.'

He raised a black winged brow. 'Interrogated?'

'What else would you call it?'

'Perhaps if you'd told me the truth to start with…'

'I haven't told you any lies.'

'I'm satisfied that you've told me the truth *as far as it goes*. But I'm not a complete fool. I know you've been out with David.'

Then, surprising her, 'From the description you gave me of your husband, I imagine my brother is a lot like him?'

'Yes,' she admitted.

'Well, just bear in mind that, unlike your husband, David's a philanderer, a heartbreaker.'

'How kind of you to warn me.'

'So where did he take you?' The question came with the suddenness of an ambush.

'I've already said I won't answer any more questions.'

'As a matter of fact you don't need to; I can guess. You see, I'm well aware that David keeps a room at the Trans Luxor, over on the Lido… And the fact that your hair is loose suggests that you've either been swimming or indulging in some…shall we say…*indoor* exercise…'

Watching her eyes drop in confusion, and her cheeks grow hot, he remarked trenchantly, 'I can see I've guessed right. So which form did the exercise take?'

'As it's nothing to do with you, I've no intention of telling you.'

'I suppose I don't need to ask. David is no slouch when it comes to getting women into bed.'

'Neither is his brother,' she retorted. 'And at least David isn't engaged...'

As soon as the remark was out she wished it unsaid.

His grey eyes narrowing, Dominic queried, 'So what exactly did he tell you?'

Trying to sound as though she didn't care, she said, 'Only that you were going to be married.'

Then suddenly the pain and bitterness overflowed. 'I can quite understand why you want both the ring and Ca' Malvasia back.' Blinded by tears, she jumped to her feet and headed for the door.

He got there ahead of her and, his back to the panels, stood blocking the way.

'Don't rush off.'

Head bent, struggling to hold back the tears, she said thickly, 'Please let me leave.'

'Not until you tell me whether or not you went to bed with David.'

Lifting her head, the tears pouring down her cheeks, she cried fiercely, 'Why bother asking? If I denied it, you wouldn't believe me.'

'Try me.'

'Of course I went to bed with him! Knowing the sort of woman I am, what else would you expect?'

'But I *don't* know. I'm still trying to find out.'

'What does it matter? So long as you get everything back you regard as yours!' Sobbing now, she tried to open the door.

When he moved, she thought he was going to let her go, but instead he pulled her into his arms.

For a few seconds she attempted futilely to free herself then, giving up the struggle, she buried her face against his chest and proceeded to cry her heart out while he held her close and stroked her hair.

'Don't upset yourself,' he said softly. 'Everything will be all right, I promise…'

But he was going to marry a woman named Carla and nothing would ever be right again.

'Now, don't cry any more.'

Struggling for control, she drew back a little, and said with pathetic dignity, 'I'm sorry.'

'There's nothing to be sorry for.' Lifting her face, he wiped away the tears with his thumb.

That tender little gesture was her undoing. Fresh tears overflowed and ran down her cheeks.

Whispering, *'Cara mia,'* he pulled her close again, and began to kiss them away.

The yearning for him, the need she felt deep inside, began to grow, and with no reserves of strength left to fight it she was lost long before his kisses changed from being merely comforting to passionate and demanding.

When Nicola opened her eyes, the room, with its white-walled simplicity, looked totally strange—until she remembered that this was Dominic's room, and, though she was alone, this was Dominic's bed she was lying in.

He had called her *cara mia*…

But he shouldn't have done. He was engaged to be married.

She gave a little moan of anguish and despair. In spite of knowing that, she had allowed herself to go to bed with him yet again.

Would she never learn?

While she was deeply and passionately in love with him, Dominic cared nothing for her. He was simply assuaging his sexual needs while he waited to marry another woman.

No, that was hardly fair. She was making it sound as if he had simply *used* her. But, a lover of great tenderness and passion, he had given her a lot more than he had asked in return.

Remembering how he had spent half the night making sweetly inventive love to her, she shivered with pleasure.

Yet while she found their physical relationship infinitely and endlessly enjoyable, it was *loving* him that lit up her whole being, *loving* him that *mattered*.

But there was no hope of Dominic loving her. Though he'd been willing to take her to bed, his main interest was getting back the ring and Ca' Malvasia to facilitate his marriage.

Knowing and accepting that, to stay here would only be torturing herself. The sooner she left for England, the better. But first she would go to see Signor Mancini and take steps to formally hand back what she now realised John should never have left her in the first place. Then she would be able to leave Venice with a clear conscience.

CHAPTER TEN

HAVING reached a decision, though her heart bled at the prospect of never seeing Dominic again, she felt a little easier in her mind.

A glance at her watch showed it was almost eleven-thirty. If she was able to make an appointment to see the solicitor this morning, she could be heading out of Venice by early afternoon.

Getting out of bed and discovering the rest had improved her ankle enormously, she gathered up her clothes, which had been placed on a carved wooden chest, and hurried into her own room.

The solicitor's phone number was in her handbag, and Nicola forced herself to pick up the phone and ring his office.

When Nicola had given her name and mentioned that the matter was urgent, his secretary informed her that, though he was going out shortly, he would make time to see her if she could come over immediately.

While she showered and dressed as quickly as possible, her mind went back over the events of the previous night.

With a feeling of shame she recalled how, when Dominic had asked her if she had slept with his brother, beside herself, she'd lied and said she had.

Now, bitterly regretting her stupidity, she wished for David's sake that she had simply denied ever being with him. If he had got into serious trouble she would be to blame.

As soon as she was ready Nicola made her way down the grand staircase in fear and trembling. The last thing she wanted to do was run into Dominic. Though hopefully, at this time of day, he would be working.

To her great relief she reached the handsome front door and closed it behind her without having encountered a soul.

Outside the sun was shining from a blue, blue sky, and the air was filled with a golden warmth that lay on her bare arms like a caress.

When she had walked the comparatively short distance to the Grand Canal, she took a water-taxi to Calle Pino, where Signor Mancini had his offices.

The middle-aged driver was cheerful and garrulous and, saying she would only be a few minutes, she asked him to wait.

A board on the door of number *sette* informed any interested persons that the offices of Mancini and Coducci were on the second floor.

Nicola rang the appropriate bell and spoke her name into a small oblong grille. In response there was a slight crackle, and a tinny voice asked her to come straight up.

A second later, with a metallic click, the bolt was released and the door swung open a few inches.

The entrance hall was dark, and she reached to press the glowing light switch before closing the door behind her and climbing the marble stairs.

Signor Mancini, a short, silver-haired, dapper man, was waiting at the door to greet her with an outstretched hand and a great many cordial remarks, and lead her into his office.

Ignoring both the hand and the pleasantries, she gave him a cool, *'Buon giorno.'*

As soon as she was seated, he queried, 'How may I help you?'

Without hesitation, she told him exactly what she had decided.

'Everything?' He sounded startled.

'Everything,' she said firmly.

'Well, of course, if that's what you wish…?'

'It is.'

'Then I'll take the necessary steps to make it legal. Will you be remaining in Venice?'

'No, I'm leaving this afternoon.'

'Where can I contact you?'

'I'm not sure. I'll have to let you know.'

Wasting no more time, she rose to her feet, and headed for the door.

When they got back to the *palazzo* she directed the taxi-driver to the tradesmen's entrance, and again asked him to wait.

Once more her luck was in and she saw no one as she hastened up the back stairs. Her cases had been stowed at the bottom of the cavernous wardrobe and, having unearthed them, she placed them on the bed and started to pack her belongings.

Nicola was about to put her grandmother's jewellery box into the smaller case when she remembered the Maschera ring. She would leave that with a note for Dominic, she decided, telling him what she had done and wishing him every happiness.

Lifting the lid, she found the chamois pouch, but it only took a second to confirm that it was empty. A quick search amongst the other items failed to locate the ring.

Bitterness rising in her throat like gall, she realised that Dominic must have taken it. Either yesterday evening, when he had come to her room to check that her belongings were still there, or this morning while she lay asleep in his bed.

But, knowing how much the ring meant to him, perhaps she couldn't blame him? In his place she might well have been tempted to do the same.

Yet she knew she *wouldn't*, and she felt an acute sense of dismay and disappointment. To simply take it while her back was turned lowered him in her estimation. It wasn't the action of a man of honour.

Her hands not quite steady, she was packing the rest of her things when a knock at the door made her jump out of her skin.

Standing motionless, she held her breath, hoping against hope that it wasn't Dominic, and that whoever had knocked would presume she wasn't there and go away.

'Nicola…' It was David's voice. 'Are you there? If you are, for God's sake open the door!'

Hurrying across the room, she opened the door to find David, grey-faced and sweating, slumped against the jamb.

Shocked, she began, 'What on earth…?'

'Listen,' he said urgently, 'I want you to do something for me…'

'Hadn't you better come in and sit down?'

'No time. I must get back before they miss me. The doctor has just diagnosed acute appendicitis…'

So he hadn't been lying about the stomach pains.

'An ambulance is coming any minute to take me into hospital, and I badly need your help.'

'What do you want me to do?'

Biting back a groan, he said, 'I want you to go to Club Nove *straight away*. Ring the bell until someone comes. Tell them your name, and insist on speaking to Angelo in person…'

Thrusting a small, brown padded envelope into her hand, he went on, 'Give him this message and tell him I've sent it.'

'Oh, but I'm just—'

'Believe me, I wouldn't ask you to do it if I wasn't desperate. But Angelo won't waste any time. If he doesn't hear from me before three o'clock he'll send his thugs after me and I'll end up in the hospital's mortuary rather than the recovery room. Please, Nicola… You're my only hope.'

Reacting to the desperation in his voice, she agreed, 'All right, I'll do it.'

He nodded and, bent over in agony, his lip caught between his teeth, began to make his slow, shuffling way down the corridor.

Afraid he would collapse, she watched him until he reached the end. Then, thankful she had a taxi waiting, she thrust the package into her bag and hurried down the back stairs. On the way she passed a maid, who gave her a curious glance but said nothing. When the driver had helped her into the boat, she told him where she wanted to go, the engine roared into life, and a moment later they were heading up the Rio dei Cavalli. As they reached the Grand Canal a water-ambulance passed them, speeding towards the *palazzo*.

As soon as she was safely away from Venice, Nicola promised herself, she would ring the hospital and make sure David was all right.

When they reached the bottom of the alleyway that led to Campo Mandolo, she gave the driver a substantial tip and said, 'If you wouldn't mind waiting again, I'll only be a few minutes. Then, when I've picked up my luggage from the *palazzo*, I'd like you to take me to Piazzale Roma.'

'Certainly, *signorina*. You're leaving Venice?'

'*Sì.*'

'You don't like our beautiful city?'

'Yes, I love it. I'll be very sad to leave.'

'Then you must come back soon.'

She managed a smile, and accepted his steadying hand as she disembarked.

The nearby restaurant was still busy with lunchtime customers as she approached the club's black studded door and rang the bell.

Inside, apart from the noise of the bell, which echoed hollowly, everything seemed quiet and deserted.

After perhaps half a minute she tried again, without success.

What was she to do if nobody came? If she failed to
deliver the package before three o'clock would David's life
really be at risk? Or had he been exaggerating?

Recalling the two men who had bundled him down the
alleyway the previous night, she knew she couldn't afford
to take any chances.

With renewed determination, she rang the bell a third
time. Somewhere inside a door banged, and a few seconds
later a tough-looking face appeared at the grille. It was the
same man who had admitted them the previous night.

'I'd like to speak to Angelo,' she said steadily.

Sounding none too pleased, the man informed her, 'He
always has a sleep after lunch.'

'I must speak to him,' she insisted. 'My name is Nicola
Whitney. I have an important message for him.'

Dark, close-set eyes studied her distrustfully, and she
thought he was going to refuse.

'Molto importante,' she stressed.

'Very well,' he growled. 'But he won't like being disturbed.'

Opening the door, he led the way across the bare foyer
and up the stairs.

'Wait in here.' He unlocked a door to the left and, switching on the light, showed her into a small windowless office.

A moment later he had closed and locked the door behind
her.

Resolved to stay calm, she took the envelope from her
bag and looked around her while she waited. There were
several grey metal filing cabinets, a cluttered desk with a
sagging leather chair, an overflowing wastepaper basket, and
a large, heavy-looking safe. The air was stale and smelled
of cigarette smoke.

The lack of windows made her feel claustrophobic, and

as the seconds ticked past she found herself gripping the padded envelope tightly, feeling a growing nervousness.

It seemed too bulky to contain just a message...

Nicola was never sure when the suspicion entered her head, but suddenly it was there.

She recalled the little scene in the alleyway—David saying, 'But I *have* got money... I just can't get my hands on it at the moment.'

And the spokesman insisting, 'Then you'd better find some other way to pay...'

What if it was David who had taken the ring?

No, no, she couldn't believe he would take the priceless Maschera ring to pay his gambling debts...

Or would he? He was almost certainly desperate enough. And after their conversation in Il Faraone he had known exactly where to find it.

Could she bring herself to look inside the package and make sure?

If she didn't, Dominic might lose one of the things he treasured most, and it would be her fault.

With sudden determination she tore open the envelope. Inside was a message scrawled on a sheet of thick white paper, and a gleaming gold ring.

As she stared at it in horror she became aware of approaching footsteps, and an instant later she heard the key turn in the lock.

If Angelo didn't know what David was sending him, she might be able to brazen it out.

Her mind working like lightning, she thrust the package down the side of the wastepaper basket to hide it, and straightened up just as the door opened.

The man who came in was of medium height, with a thin, swarthy face and a hooked nose. It was undoubtedly the same man that David had taken such care to avoid.

And all at once Nicola understood why.

Though Angelo's appearance was almost weedy, there was something repellent about him, an air of cold ruthlessness that sent a shiver down her spine.

Fixing her with glittering black eyes, he said politely, *'Buona sera.'*

'Buona sera, signor.'

'You're Signorina Whitney, I understand?'

'Signora,' she said firmly.

'You have a message for me?'

'Si Signor, from David Loredan. He was unable to come himself. Unfortunately he has just been taken into hospital with acute appendicitis.'

'I would have thought David had too much respect for me to offer weak excuses.'

'It's no excuse, *signor.'*

The deep-set eyes narrowed. 'Why did he send you just to tell me that?' With a kind of grim humour, he added, 'Surely he doesn't expect me to send him a bunch of grapes?'

She smiled slightly. 'He was afraid that if you didn't know the true situation you might be tempted to act...shall we say...hastily... All he needs is a little more time.'

'He's been saying that for weeks.'

'Though David is a wealthy man, because of a proviso in his mother's will he's having a problem actually getting hold of his money.'

His voice almost a purr, Angelo said, 'I understood he was finding some other way to pay.'

Nicola's blood ran cold.

When she said nothing, Angelo demanded, 'So what is this "other way"?'

Drawing a deep breath, she said evenly, 'I'm afraid I don't know. With David being taken ill so suddenly we had little time to talk. He might have been planning to ask his brother for help.'

'From what I've heard Dominic Loredan is seriously displeased with David's profligate ways, and this time might well refuse.'

This time… So Dominic had bailed David out in the past.

Striving to sound confident, she said, 'Blood is thicker than water, *signor*, and I'm sure Dominic wouldn't want to see any harm come to his brother.'

His black eyes pinning her, Angelo remarked silkily, 'Though you speak our language with charm and fluency, you are not Italian, I fancy?'

'No, I'm English.'

'How do you fit into this? Which of the two men is your lover?'

'Neither,' she denied crisply. 'I'm simply a guest at the *palazzo*.'

'For a guest, you seem to know a great deal.'

'What I *do* know is there's no lack of money there, and it would be well worth your while to give David some leeway. Once he's out of hospital I'm sure he will find a way to pay what he owes.'

Then, with a confidence she was far from feeling, 'Now, if you'll excuse me, I must be getting back. *Buona sera, signor.*'

Shaking his head, Angelo smiled mirthlessly. 'I should like you to stay. In fact I insist on it. I'm convinced the thought of you being here will speed David's…*recovery.*'

So he hadn't believed her.

Raising his voice, he called, 'Enrico.'

The door opened at once, making it quite clear that the burly man who had admitted her earlier had been waiting just outside.

'Signora Whitney will be staying for a while. Make her comfortable in the back room. But first…'

Holding out his hand and addressing Nicola, he asked politely, 'If I may?'

It took her a second or two to realise he wanted her shoulder bag.

She passed it to him without a word.

Putting the bag down on the desk, he searched through it swiftly and efficiently, obviously expecting to find the ring. He paused to check her passport and driving licence before nodding to the burly man, who seized her arm and began to propel her towards the door.

'There's no need to use force, Enrico,' Angelo observed mildly. 'I'm sure Signora Whitney won't give us any trouble.'

Wanting to beg him to let her leave, but knowing it was useless, Nicola followed Enrico back down the stairs, across the foyer, and along a short passage.

At the end of the passage a couple of steps led down to a metal door that opened into what appeared to be a storeroom.

Thrusting her inside, Enrico closed the door with a clang, and a second later a key grated in the lock.

She felt a sudden surge of panic, a desire to scream and pound on the door.

But, having got this far, she must keep her head.

Standing quite still, her hands clenched into fists, she fought off the panic, telling herself firmly that no one would do her any harm. She was merely here as a hostage, and it would only be a matter of time before she was released.

When she felt calmer, she looked around her. Her prison was small and gloomy and filled with such a variety of junk that there was hardly any floor space left.

It had no windows; the only source of light was an ornate grille set high in a brick wall that, judging by the dank smell, backed on to a canal.

Wondering if there was any chance of escape, she looked around her for something to stand on. There were several packing cases, but they all appeared too heavy to move.

A long-legged rickety stool seemed to be the answer to her prayers and, setting it down as close to the wall as the surrounding clutter allowed, she climbed on it to examine the grille.

It didn't take her long to discover that though the metal was flaky with rust it was strong and set firmly into the surrounding mortar.

No chance of escape that way.

It seemed she was fated to stay here until David had recovered enough to miss her.

Unless she could attract someone's attention.

She had been right about the canal, but the waterway appeared to be stagnant and little used, and the backs of the buildings opposite looked for all the world like semi-derelict warehouses.

As she leaned forward to try and see down the length of the canal one of the legs of the stool suddenly snapped, and she fell, scraping her face against the rough bricks of the wall and landing on a pile of junk that was anything but soft.

It took her a minute or more to collect herself and find her feet. Then, making her way rather shakily across the only litter-free bit of floor, she sat down on one of the packing cases.

There was a burning pain down one cheek. Touching it gingerly, she felt the wet stickiness of blood.

Well, it was her own fault; she should have taken more care. And, like her previous accident, it could have been a great deal worse...

As the time crawled past on leaden feet her thoughts turned to Dominic and she found herself wondering what he was doing.

Had he missed her by now?

Yesterday he had been concerned about her. But today he was probably too worried about his brother to have given her a thought. She felt sure that, no matter how much trouble David had caused him, he *would* be worried...

A sudden movement outside the door and the sound of a key being turned in the lock made her look up.

Enrico was standing there. With a jerk of his head he motioned her to follow him.

Feeling bruised and stiff, she obeyed.

As they approached the office she heard Angelo saying, '...owes me a great deal of money.'

Then a low, attractive voice answering, 'When I'm satisfied that Signora Whitney is here and unharmed, I'll be prepared to discuss the matter with you.'

Enrico opened the door and propelled her forward. She stumbled into the room to find Angelo by the desk, facing a grim-looking Dominic.

She was wondering how he'd managed to find her so quickly when, taking in her battered appearance, he exclaimed, 'Dear God!'

'It's all right,' Nicola assured him hurriedly, as a white line appeared round his mouth. 'It was an accident.'

Seeing he wasn't convinced, she explained, 'I climbed on a stool to try and see through the grille. One of the legs broke, and I scraped my face on the wall...'

'They haven't hurt you in any way? Because if they have—'

'No... No, they haven't,' she assured him. 'I'm fine.' But her relief was so great at having Dominic there that though she tried very hard to appear totally composed she began to tremble.

Putting an arm around her, he announced with quiet authority, 'I'm taking Signora Whitney straight home. I'll see you tomorrow morning at ten o'clock.'

Angelo looked at him, weighing him up, then warned, 'It wouldn't pay to change your mind.'

'I'm not in the habit of changing my mind,' Dominic told him curtly.

'I'd like my bag, please.' Nicola was surprised by how normal her voice sounded.

'Of course,' Angelo said smoothly, and passed it to her.

Without another word Dominic escorted her out of the building and down the alleyway to where his motorboat was waiting by the water-lapped steps, moored to an iron ring.

Only then did she remember how she'd got there. 'I came by water-taxi and I asked the driver to wait...'

'Yes. When you didn't reappear, he had the good sense to come back to the *palazzo*. Thank the Lord I'd just returned from the hospital, and when he mentioned Campo Mandolo I realised where you must have gone, and at whose instigation.'

He looked so cold and angry that, biting her lip, Nicola relapsed into silence, and the rest of the journey back was made without a word being spoken.

When they reached Palazzo dei Cavalli he led her straight to his study and settled her on the couch. 'How long is it since you had anything to eat? Did you have any lunch?'

She shook her head.

'I'll get Maria to bring you something. A bowl of soup, perhaps?'

Her stomach churning, she said, 'I don't think I can eat anything just yet.'

'Very well.'

He disappeared into the bathroom to return after a moment or two with a small bowl and a first-aid box. Bending over her, he began to bathe her cheek.

Though his face was hard and set, his hands were as gentle and tender as a caress.

Tending to her injuries was getting to be a habit, she thought with wry humour, then winced as the antiseptic stung her raw cheek.

Pausing, he asked, 'Is it very painful?'

'No, not at all,' she mumbled, and saw a muscle in his jaw jerk.

He finished his ministrations by spreading on a fine layer of soothing ointment.

'Thank you,' she said. 'That feels a lot better.'

By the time he'd cleared away the things he'd been using, and dropped into a seat opposite, it was hardly hurting at all.

She had expected him to start questioning her, and had psyched herself up to answer, but, tight-lipped and oddly pale beneath his tan, he sat in brooding silence staring blindly at the floor.

Dismayed by his attitude, and with the strain of the day beginning to tell, she was finding it difficult to control her emotions.

Needing to be alone, she rose a shade unsteadily and said, 'If you don't mind I'd like to lie down for a while...'

He looked up, and she was shocked by the bleakness of his expression.

'I—I'm sorry you're so angry with me,' she stammered.

'It's not you I'm angry with. It's that idiot brother of mine for putting you at risk.'

He jumped to his feet, and a moment later she was in his arms, being held close.

She was amazed to find that Dominic—strong, imperturbable Dominic—was trembling.

His cheek pressed against her hair, he whispered, 'Dear God, if anything had happened to you... I don't know what I would have done.'

As his arms tightened convulsively, she gave a little gasp.

'I'm sorry, did I hurt you?'

'No... No, you didn't...'

But already he was drawing back.

'Dominic, I...' Only too happy to be in his arms, but

suddenly remembering Carla and unable to tell him so, she broke off in some confusion.

Once more in command of himself, he said evenly, 'Before you go, I want to ask you something. Why did you decide to leave without even telling me? Was it because of what happened last night?'

'Partly,' she admitted.

'What made you go to see your solicitor?'

'How did you—?'

'He phoned just as I was leaving to find you, and told me what you were proposing to do. I want to know why.'

As levelly as possible, she said, 'Because I've come to realise I have no right to things that morally belong to the Loredan family.'

'I must admit that was how I first thought of it. But now *I've* come to realise I was wrong. Therefore I've asked Signor Mancini to ignore your instructions.'

Sinking back onto the couch, she protested, 'But surely you want Ca' Malvasia back?'

'If you're willing to sell, I'll be happy to buy it back at the market price.'

'And the ring?'

His smile wry and self-mocking, he said, 'Though it may sound foolish, I'd always visualised giving the Maschera ring to the woman I loved and intended to marry...' After a moment, he went on, 'David was rambling just before they sedated him. He kept saying I should stop you taking it...'

She caught her breath. It sounded as if he had had second thoughts...

'So presumably you told him you were leaving?'

When, uncertain how to answer, she hesitated, Dominic said, 'Look, I know he came up to your room...' Then, urgently, 'It crossed my mind that you might have fallen in love with him?'

'No, I haven't fallen in love with him.'

She heard Dominic's sigh of relief.

'But you said he was like Jeff. You admitted you'd slept with him...'

'He *is* like Jeff, at least in looks. But I didn't sleep with him.'

'Thank heaven for that!'

'I only said I did because I was so upset.'

'Why were you so upset?'

'I didn't like the idea that for the past two nights I'd made love to someone else's fiancé.'

'But you did it again,' he pointed out quietly.

Flushing, she said, 'That's why I'm leaving.'

'I see. Would it make any difference to your decision if I told you that I had no intention of marrying Carla?'

When, hardly daring to hope, she waited, her eyes fixed on his face, he went on, 'I wanted to settle down, to have a wife and a family, but I seemed unable to find the woman of my dreams. Carla's a beautiful girl, and I'm fond of her, so eventually we drifted into an engagement. I might even have married her if I hadn't discovered, quite by chance, that she was in love with David.

'She has her pride, and she begged me to keep it a secret and just let things drift for a while... I agreed, though from odd things David has let drop I rather suspect that the interest might be mutual...'

Remembering their conversation in the restaurant, Nicola said, 'I'm sure you're right.'

'And of course they're more of an age,' Dominic pursued. 'Though if Carla does decide to take on that graceless young scamp she'll need to keep him firmly in order...'

'Won't her mother object?'

A shade cynically, he told her, 'I imagine that Signora Ferrini, who has a soft spot for David, would happily swap one Loredan for another. He may even be able to persuade her to move to the States. Which wouldn't be a bad thing.

It might keep him out of the clutches of men like Angelo
Gallo…

'And, speaking of Gallo, would you like to tell me exactly
what happened today? Why David sent you?'

'He wanted me to take…a message.'

'A message? Why couldn't he have phoned?'

Her mind going a total blank, she said nothing.

'So the message wasn't a verbal one?'

'No. An envelope.'

Sounding as if he was thinking aloud, Dominic said,
'Why go to the trouble of sending a note? Why not an e-
mail or a text message? Unless there was something else in
the envelope…'

He was too clever by half, she thought, trying to look
calm and failing dismally.

His sharp eyes noting her confusion, he said, 'And presumably you know what that something was?'

'Yes,' she said reluctantly.

'Well?'

'Oh, can't you ask David?'

'I'm asking you. And I want an answer.'

Hating herself, she admitted, 'It was the Maschera ring.'

'You *gave* it to him?' Dominic demanded incredulously.

'No. He knew where it was and he must have taken it. I
discovered it was missing as I was packing. I'd intended to
leave it for you.'

Dominic groaned. 'No wonder Gallo let us go so easily.
I'd willingly have paid him, but now he has the ring—'

Nicola shook her head. 'He hasn't.'

'What do you mean, he hasn't?'

'The envelope David gave me was quite thickly padded,
which seemed unnecessary for just a message, and while I
was waiting in Angelo's office I began to get suspicious…'

As steadily as possible she explained how she had opened

the package and disposed of it when she heard someone coming, and what she had told Angelo.

'So that's why he kept you, to put pressure on David... And unless he's come across it the ring's still stuffed behind his wastepaper basket...'

'No. When I got rid of the note and the envelope I kept the ring.'

'You kept the ring?' Dominic echoed incredulously. 'How did you manage to hide it?'

'I wore it,' she said simply, and held out her left hand. The mask was turned into her palm, the back of her hand showing only an innocent gold band on her wedding finger.

Lifting her hand to his lips, he kissed it. 'You're not only beautiful and courageous, you're very clever.'

Warmed by his praise, she slipped off the ring and gave it to him.

His eyes on her face, he asked, 'Don't you like it? Wouldn't you prefer to keep it?'

She shook her head. 'I can't. It's a beautiful ring and I love it, but it isn't really mine to keep. John should never have given it to me.'

'What if *I* gave it to you?'

'But you should give it to the woman you marry.'

'So you want me to propose first?'

Feeling as though her throat was full of shards of hot glass, she begged, 'Please don't joke about it.'

'I've never felt less like joking. Will you marry me, Nicola?'

Unable to believe what she was hearing, she simply gaped at him.

'I know it's sudden, but I also know that you're the woman I've been waiting for. In spite of believing the worst, I fell in love with you the minute I saw you...'

When, choked by happiness, she continued to stare silently at him, he said slowly, 'I had hoped you might be able to forgive the way I've treated you... I'd even dared to hope that you might feel something more than mere attraction for me... But it seems I was wrong.'

She found her voice. 'No, you weren't wrong. I knew from the start that I loved you, that you were special.'

'Cara mia,' he whispered, and, sitting beside her, slipped the ring back on her finger.

Then, gathering her into his arms, he began to kiss her with a tender passion that melted her heart and more than made up for the times she'd been miserable.

After a while he raised his head to complain, 'When I asked why you'd slept with me, you didn't say anything about my being special.'

'I couldn't.'

'Because of what I'd said about John?'

'Yes. You see John *was* special, but in a totally different way. He was a friend, never a lover.'

'Why do you think he bequeathed everything, including the ring, to you? Was it to spite the Loredans?'

'I'm still not sure,' she admitted honestly. 'I hope it was just because he liked me. All he said in the letter he left was that he wanted me to have it.'

'Did you keep the letter?'

'Yes.' She reached for her bag and, after feeling in the zipped compartment, passed the letter to him.

While she watched him, he read what his stepfather had written.

Nicola, my dear, though we've known each other just a short time, you've been like the daughter I always wanted, and your warmth and kindness have meant a lot to me.

In the pouch you'll find Sophia's ring. Since she died I've been wearing it on a chain around my neck, but now I sense that I haven't got much longer, so I'm lodging it with Mr Harthill.

It's a singular ring. My darling always wore it. She was wearing it the day I met her. She once remarked that if any ring possessed the power to bring its wearer happiness, this one does. For that reason I would like you to have it, and I truly believe Sophia would approve.

Though we had both been married before, she was the love of my life as, I hope and believe, I was hers. We were very happy together for five wonderful years. Not long enough. But perhaps it never is.

In your case, I know your time with your husband was very brief. You're desperately young to have known so much grief and pain, and I'm only too aware that anyone who loses a loved one needs time to mourn. But remember, my dear, no one should mourn for ever. It's time you moved on. Be happy.

John

When he had finished reading it, Dominic passed it back and said slowly, 'I owe you an abject apology. As soon as I began to get to know you I felt I'd been wrong about you. But I had to keep pushing to be certain…' He sighed. 'I've given you a hard time. I just wish there was something I could do to make up for it.'

Greatly daring, she said, 'Well, there is one thing…'

'What's that, *cara mia*?'

'Tomorrow morning it would be nice to wake up with you in bed beside me.'

His white teeth gleamed in a smile. 'Consider it done. Though it might mean putting Gallo off until the afternoon… On the other hand, if I go and see him as arranged you could always stay in bed and wait for me.'

'What a wonderful idea.'

He kissed her, and asked, 'How do you feel?'

'Fine. Why?'

'I thought if you still want to lie down I might come with you.'

She pretended to consider the matter. 'Well, because of my bruises I'm sure I'll be more comfortable lying down than sitting.'

'Then what are we waiting for?'

'Suppose Maria catches us?'

'If she does, I'll leave it to you to smooth her ruffled feathers.'

'And how would you suggest I do that?'

Straightfaced, he suggested, 'You could always ask her to be bridesmaid.'

Harlequin Romance ®

Delightful
Affectionate
Romantic
Emotional

Tender
Original

Daring
Riveting
Enchanting
Adventurous
Moving

Harlequin Romance ® —
capturing the world you dream of...

...there's more to the story!

Superromance.
A *big* satisfying read about unforgettable
characters. Each month we offer *six* very different
stories that range from family drama to adventure
and mystery, from highly emotional stories to
romantic comedies—and much more! Stories
about people you'll believe in and care about.
Stories too compelling to put down....

Our authors are among today's *best* romance
writers. You'll find familiar names and talented
newcomers. Many of them are award winners—
and you'll see why!

If you want the biggest and best
in romance fiction, you'll get it
from Superromance!

Emotional, Exciting, Unexpected...

HARLEQUIN®
INTRIGUE

WE'LL LEAVE YOU BREATHLESS!

If you've been looking for thrilling tales of
contemporary passion and sensuous love stories
with taut, edge-of-the-seat suspense—then
you'll love Harlequin Intrigue!

Every month, you'll meet four new heroes
who are guaranteed to make your spine tingle
and your pulse pound. With them you'll enter
into the exciting world of Harlequin Intrigue—
where your life is on the line
and so is your heart!

THAT'S INTRIGUE—
ROMANTIC SUSPENSE
AT ITS BEST!

Harlequin® Historical

From rugged lawmen and valiant knights to defiant heiresses and spirited frontierswomen, Harlequin Historicals will capture your imagination with their dramatic scope, passion and adventure.

Harlequin Historicals...
they're too good to miss!